THE EVIL BELOW

'*Investigator seeks secretary, amanuensis, and general assistant. Applicant must exhibit courage, strength, willingness to take risks and explore the unknown . . .* ' In 1905, John O'Leary had newly arrived in San Francisco. Looking for work, he had answered the advert, little understanding what was required for the post — he'd try anything once. In America he found a world of excitement and danger . . . and working for Abraham ben Zaccheus, San Francisco's most famous psychic detective, there was never a dull moment . . .

Books by Richard A. Lupoff
in the Linford Mystery Library:

THE UNIVERSAL HOLMES
THE CASES OF CHASE
AND DELACROIX
ONE MURDER AT A TIME

RICHARD A. LUPOFF

————————◆————————

THE EVIL
BELOW

DETECTIVE MYSTERY STORIES

Complete and Unabridged

LINFORD
Leicester

First published in Great Britain

First Linford Edition
published 2013

Copyright © 2009, 2011 by Richard A. Lupoff

British Library CIP Data

Lupoff, Richard A., *1935 –*
    The evil below. - -
    (Linford mystery library)
    1. Detective and mystery stories.
    2. Large type books.
    I. Title II. Series
    813.5′4–dc23

    ISBN 978–1–4448–1401–9

Published by
F. A. Thorpe (Publishing)
Anstey, Leicestershire

Set by Words & Graphics Ltd.
Anstey, Leicestershire
Printed and bound in Great Britain by
T. J. International Ltd., Padstow, Cornwall

This book is printed on acid-free paper

Hebrews Have No Horns

When I was an altar boy back in Kilkee, Father Phinean warned us to watch out for Hebrews who would try and steal our immortal souls. Failing that, their favorite trick was to steal good Christian babies and grind their bones to make their *matzie* crackers and drink their blood at their Passover *sadie* parties. I once asked the Father if Our Lord hadn't told his blessed disciples to eat His Holy Flesh and drink His Holy Blood at the last Passover *sadie* He attended in Jerusalem.

For an answer Father Phinean fetched me one on the ear that made my head ring for a week and left me with a cauliflower ear that's been my blessing ever since I came to America. That was the last time I saw the inside of St. Padraic's Church, you can be certain, and the last that St. Padraic's would ever see of John O'Leary. Ah, but with my cauliflower ear all I need to do is stroll

1

into a saloon and swagger up to the mahogany and the boys all think I'm a pugilist and my drinks are on the house or else somebody decides to show he's a better man than I am and I get to engage in a lovely brawl and then I have my drinks afterward.

But the day came when I had to leave Kilkee in a hurry and wound up in Five Points in New York City just in time to welcome in the Twentieth Century. I gradually found my way across this whole wide continent and wound up here in San Francisco with nowhere farther west to go unless I wanted to visit China. Which, come to think of it, might be an interesting experience indeed, indeed. But I'm not inclined to try that out quite yet. Mayhap a few years hence.

But here it is close to Advent in this Year of Our Lord 1905 and here I am in this lovely city in this lovely country and if they miss me in Ireland as much as I miss them then they don't miss me at all. Not at all.

Which is not to deny that I had dear friends in Kilkee. I grew up fighting and playing with Shane Galloway and Rogan Doherty and Seamus McCarthy and Malachy Teague, and chasing after Glenna Lynch and pulling her pigtails and falling in love with sweet Maeve Corrigan. Sweet Maeve with her hair the color of flame and her eyes the color of Ireland's green fields and her skin like soft, virgin snow. Dear Maeve, kicked dead by an Englishman's fancy riding horse at the age of twelve. To this day I can smell the incense burned at her obsequies. If Maeve were living I'd have stayed in Kilkee forever. Stayed there with Maeve else left with her in my arms. But with Maeve dead Kilkee will see no more of John O'Leary.

What a wonderful land this America is. I worked as a fireman, of all things, in New York. I hefted barrels in a brewery in Chicago. I was a plasterer in St. Louis and I went down in a copper mine to earn my bread and cheese in Colorado. And when I arrived in San Francisco I decided to try something new. I am very fond of new things.

I picked up a copy of the San Francisco

Daily Morning Call that some gent had left behind in a saloon shortly after I arrived in this fine city. The newspapers of any city provide a useful introduction, I have found, and this one was full of unpleasant details about assorted murders, robberies, and political scandals. Ah, well, I said to myself, so this fine town is no different from the other metropolises of the New World.

I still had a few coins in my pocket and betwixt free hardboiled eggs with my beer and a little labor picking up merchandise that fell off the backs of drays coming from the harbor I had no problem keeping body and soul together here in San Francisco. But I did have the itch, and so I turned the pages of that newspaper looking for advertisements by employers looking for workers and I found one that interested me indeed.

It was posted by one Mr. Abraham ben Zaccheus and listed an address in the neighborhood they call Rooshian Hill. Here's what it said:

INVESTIGATOR seeks secretary, amanuensis, and general assistant. Something is happening in the Earth. Something is going to happen. Applicant must exhibit courage, strength, willingness to take risks and explore the unknown. Keen olfactory and kinetic senses vital. Room, board, and salary provided. Apply in person only.

*　*　*

I read the advertisement over a number of times. Courage, strength, willingness to take risks and explore the unknown, eh? Why, if that didn't describe John O'Leary, formerly of Kilkee, County Clare, Ireland, to a T, I would still be living in Kilkee, upsetting Father Phinean with my impertinent questions and getting walloped alongside my noggin for my trouble.

As for something happening in the Earth, oh, that could mean anything or nothing. Maybe there was another volcano preparing to explode. Oh, yes, we hear about such things, even in Kilkee. I once owned a book with a picture of Krakatoa in it, and a description of the eruption of that monstrous beast in 1883, a mere twenty-two years ago. Why, I was already a lad studying my letters and interrupting Father at Mass in that remembered year. And of course there was Vesuvius that buried the wicked Romans back in the year 79 *anno domini*. I wonder, now, did the lava and dust kill all the worshippers of Jupiter and the other heathen gods in old Pompei, and spare the holy Christians? I have my doubts. Ah, but the Father would be after me with his fists if he could hear me now!

I will confess that the requirement for keen olfactory and kinetic senses left me at a loss, but I know that I have horse sense, at least, and I was willing to bluff my way through those others if the need should arise.

Thus I hied myself up Rooshian Hill and located Mr. ben Zaccheus's address, which was that of a pleasant looking residence of no great pretentiousness. The windows were large and the roof was decorated with the curlicues the local folks hereabouts call gingerbread. It was distinguished, I noticed, by an odd little gadget that was nailed to the doorpost but I didn't know what it was so I went ahead and knocked on the door.

The sky had got dark and there was a cold, wet wind ruffling my hair and starting to spatter my dear cheeks, which caused me to wish that either the personage who had placed the advertisement would admit me to his august presence, or that a servant would appear to do as much.

The fellow who opened the door looked ordinary enough. He had a beard but they're commonly seen in San Francisco, although I like to keep my own face shaved so I can show it off. Not that I'm conceited but I'll admit that I am good-looking. He was shorter than I am and did not look lean nor hungry. I saw that he was wearing a little skull-cap like the biretta a Monsignor would wear and I was thinking that he might be some kind of Greek or Rooshian Father with that skull cap and that name and that beard.

He smiled at me and said something like, 'Saloon.' I don't think that was what he said, but it was as close as I could make out. I said it back to him, as close as

I could come, and he seemed pleased and took a step backward and made a gesture with his hand and I felt almost as if something picked me up and carried me into the house.

He closed the door behind me and gestured again and I found myself sitting on an overstuffed sofa.

First chance I got, I asked if he was a Greek or Rooshian Father. You won't believe me but I remember exactly how he replied because it knocked me for a loop.

'No,' said the gentleman in question, 'I am not Greek and I am not Rooshian. I am an American but before I was an American I was a subject of — '

And then he told me and it was like the sweet poetry of Ireland. I just listened admiringly at the moment, but later I asked him to write it down for me and he did. Here is what he wrote down:

'I was a subject of His Imperial and Apostolic Majesty, Franz Joseph I, by the Grace of God, Emperor of Austria, King of Hungary and Bohemia, King of Lombardy and Venice, of Dalmatia,

Croatia, Slavonia, Lodomeria and Illyria; King of Jerusalem, Archduke of Austria, Grand Duke of Tuscany and Kraków, Duke of Lorraine, of Salzburg, Styria, Carinthia, Carniola and of the Bukovina; Grand Prince of Transylvania; Margrave of Moravia; Duke of Upper and Lower Silesia, of Modena, Parma, Piacenza and Guastalla, of Oświęcim and Zator, of Cieszyn, Friuli, Ragusa and Zadar; Princely Count of Habsburg and Tyrol, of Kyburg, Gorizia and Gradisca; Prince of Trento and Brixen; Margrave of Upper and Lower Lusatia and Istria; Count of Hohenems, Feldkirch, Bregenz, Sonnenberg, Lord of Trieste, of Kotor, and the Wendish Mark, and Grand Voivode of the Voivodina of Serbia.'

'Holy Mother of God,' I exclaimed, falling to my knees, 'I didn't know, your highness.'

The gentleman guffawed and put his hand on my shoulder. I thought he was going to declare me a royal knight of the kingdom but all he did was laugh at me.

'Get up,' he said. 'Get up, my fine man. Those titles belonged to another fellow who lives far away in Vienna, where I was born too, but in my father's humble house, not in a splendid palace like the Emperor.'

'You're not a king, then?' I asked.

He laughed again and said that he was not, and would I please be so kind as to get up off his carpet and drink a glass of tea and eat some cake.

Well, I am not a great lover of that particular beverage but I did not want to offend this king. I still thought mayhap he was a king in disguise, you see, but he was not. He was, he told me, Mr. Abraham ben Zaccheus, which I already knew as that was the name in his newspaper advertisement, and he was a gentleman of the Hebrew persuasion, he told me, which I found harder to believe than that he was not a king because he had no horns, you see. Not even little ones.

Oh, I wish he had come to Kilkee so the Father there could see that Hebrews have no horns. That set me to thinking. If the Father could be wrong about one thing, he could be wrong about other things, don't you see? And if Mr.

Abraham ben Zaccheus had no horns, then mayhap he did not grind the bones of Christian babies to make his *matzie* crackers nor drink their blood in his Passover *sadies*.

Oh, this New World was a wondrous place, and San Francisco was a most wondrous city!

So there I sat, don't you see, in Mr. Abraham ben Zaccheus's parlor. This was a stuffy room furnished with a horsehair sofa and chairs, with brocaded hangings and a gilt-framed mirror and photographs on the walls of people looking solemn and serious that I took it to be relatives of Mr. Abraham ben Zaccheus in whatever country it was that he came from where he was not the king.

There was one photograph of an old gent in a splendid military uniform. This one was set aside from the others and I took it to be the Imperial and Apostolic Majesty and all them other things. I didn't think he could be of the Hebrew persuasion, though. I don't think that any Imperial and Apostolic Majesties have been of the Hebrew persuasion for a very long time.

My host excused himself from the room and I studied my surroundings while I awaited his return. There was a handsome spinet piano with a woven tapestry-looking cover on it, and a golden candelabrum with as many arms as one of them octopussy beasts that Mr. Verne the Frenchie writes about. The walls, where they were not covered with portraits of splendid ladies in elegant gowns and gentlemen in uniforms or dark robes, were covered with bookcases filled with leather-bound volumes. Some were stamped with titles in English; others, in foreign markings that didn't even look like good honest ABC's.

I was about to take one down when a throat was cleared behind me and there stood my bearded host with a silver tray in his hands. He set the tray down upon a table. There were two tea cups on it, each filled with a lovely looking liquid.

'You will forgive me,' the gentleman declaimed, 'but this is a test of sorts. Will you be so good as to tell me what each of these cups contains?'

I resumed my seat upon the horsehair sofa and lifted one cup, then the other. Ahah! Neither of them contained tea at all.

'This, sir,' I told my host after sniffing the contents of the tea cup, 'is Coleraine Single Malt '34' whisky, as fine a beverage as ever was created in Ireland or anywhere else upon the face of Mother Earth.' I lowered the cup and lifted its companion. *Sniff! Sniff!* 'And this, alas, is Glenmorangie Madeira Wood Finish whiskey, as good a drink as the barbaric Scots folk are capable of distilling. 'Tis fit for such as them to drink, I suppose.'

My host grinned broadly. 'Well, young man, you have passed that test with flying colors. You identified the two cups by olfactory examination alone. If you wish to drink them down, by all means do so.'

Ah, well, the Coleraine was a treat indeed, and the Glenmorangie I managed to force down solely so as not to give offense.

The gentleman disappeared once again, taking the tray and empty cups with him.

In quick time he was back, and there

was a silver pot of tea on the table before me, set there by my host with his own hands, along with fresh wedges of yellow lemon and slices of a sweet, heavy cake. I sipped at the tea, which was not at all bad although it would have benefited from a few drops of that fine Coleraine or even the poor Glenmorangie, and nibbled at the cake, thinking that if I came away from this house with naught more to show for my trouble I could drop a slice in the pocket of my jacket.

Mr. Abraham ben Zacchius removed his spectacles and — I did tell you that Mr. Abraham ben Zacchius wore thick spectacles, did I not? — and polished them with a pocket handkerchief. When he had them off he had a vague look to him that made me think that he was just about as blind as a bat, and when he put them back on they made his eyes look as big as hen's eggs.

'I assume that you have come in response to my advertisement in the San Francisco *Daily Morning Call*,' Mr. Abraham ben Zaccheus said.

I admitted that such was indeed the

case. I volunteered that my name was John O'Leary and that I hailed from the village of Kilkee in the nation of Ireland, English overlords be damned.

'Well, Mr. John O'Leary, are you a man of intelligence and education?' Mr. Abraham ben Zaccheus asked me.

I admitted that such was indeed the case.

'You can read and write?'

'Indeed, sir.'

'And are you a man of physical prowess and courage?'

'I've never backed off from a fight, sir,' I told Mr. Abraham ben Zaccheus, 'nor seldom lost one.'

The gentleman grunted at that, seemingly pleased to hear what I had to say to him.

'John,' he said to me, which familiarity I found objectionable until he followed it with, 'I hope I may call you John, and will you be so kind as to call me Abraham?'

I almost dropped my teacup, thinking that a king was asking me to call him by his Christian name, but then I realized that Abraham was not his Christian name at all, but his Hebrew name. Which of course was but little help if he truly was a king in disguise, but I said to him, 'Of course, sir, Mr. Abraham.'

'Just Abraham,' he insisted.

'Very well, sir.'

'Now, John — we do have that settled, I hope?'

'Aye, sir.'

'Now, John, it will be necessary for you to understand that mine is an unusual occupation. I travel from place to place seeking to unravel mysteries that have nonplussed the usual investigators.'

I thought about that for a bit of a while, nibbling at Abraham's cake, which was really very tasty and I was certain not made from the bones of Christian babies, and sipping at his tea, which was truthfully as excellent as it could be without the aid of a drop of Coleraine or Ballydoyl or Tyrconnell's Single Malt.

'Ahah!' I replied after a bit, 'like that Mr. Sherlock Holmes that the good Irish Doctor Doyle writes his tales about.'

'Indeed, something like that,' Abraham conceded.

'And I'm thinking,' I said, taking another sip of Abraham's excellent tea and wishing that it was a bit stronger than it was, 'that you're after hiring a fellow to be your Doctor Watson. Is that the idea you have, Abraham?' I very nearly called him Your Majesty, or King Abraham, but I held myself back, you see.

'John' said Abraham at this moment, 'you are a clever fellow and you have fathomed my intentions exactly. Of course my methods are not exactly those of the estimable Mr. Holmes, but I will need someone to accompany me on my excursions. It will be your duty to assist me as needed, and I trust to record my doings for my own referral as well as those of others, and for my posterity. For you see, John, there are times when I am not able to protect myself against — certain forces.'

Certain forces indeed, I thought, although I did not say anything at the moment. I believed that I had been fortunate indeed to pick up that copy of the San Francisco *Daily Morning Call*, and doubly so that I was the first person, mayhap the only person, to respond to Abraham's advertisement.

Abraham told me that quarters were available for my use in the rear of his home, and that a most splendid and reliable woman came in each day to keep his house in order and to prepare his meals for him. This, of course, did not startle me in the very least, for if Abraham was a kind of Californian Sherlock Holmes and I was to be his new Dr. Watson, then surely there must be a Mrs. Hudson to cook and clean.

Ah, it's a good thing, don't you see, that we learn to read and write in Kilkee. Many an Irish youth there is who doesn't know his letters, but in Kilkee the Father provides a classroom for willing lads where they learn to read and write as well as to know the Sacraments and the Commandments.

Abraham was a detective, then!

I thought, *Thou shalt not kill!*

There remained a small negotiation regarding my wages, and to my astonishment Abraham proved quite generous in that regard. As I had no possessions save the clothing in which I had arrived at Abraham's house, the gentleman provided me with two silver dollars as a small advance against my first month's wages and sent me on my way to procure some changes of raiment for myself.

I took myself on foot back down Rooshian Hill, pausing first to look out across the San Francisco Bay. Ah, if ever I felt a longing for the tors and lakes of Ireland (which I did not), I knew that I need only gaze at these glistering waters and the hills beyond to soothe my soul. The dark shapes of schooners at anchor in the Bay and the white squares and triangles of sail bellied out by a late afternoon wind added spice and vivacity to the glories of nature spreading before me. The gusty mist that had wet my face a while ago had passed, although the sky remained a pearly gray rather than blue.

It took me the shortest time to reach the emporia of Market Street and purchase a good pair of Levi Strauss's canvas trousers, a warm shirt, a mackinaw and a strong set of sturdy boots to supplement my careworn brogans. I was planning to return to Rooshian Hill and settle in for the night, but I stopped first to celebrate my good fortune at a music hall where a line of lovely young ladies disported themselves most merrily to the accompaniment of a cornet and piano.

The establishment offered a tasty selection of comestibles and a tempting array of beverages to accompany the evening's entertainment, and fortunately I had sufficient change left from Abraham's advance to purchase a good steak and a small bottle of wine. I must have looked like a swell, at least to some, and I will report with pride that I resisted the temptation to avail myself of female companionship for the evening.

As I left the establishment I was accosted by a pair of toughs. They were dressed in dark outfits with pulled-down hats. One of them was a good sight smaller than the other. I think they figured me for a dipsomaniac, which I am not, whom they could roll for his pelf, of which by now I had almost none, or possibly sell to the captain of a sailing ship to serve on his return voyage to wherever he had first parted from.

For all that I enjoy a good friendly brawl of an evening, especially after taking aboard a bit of a squiff, I am not by nature a violent man. Still, these two ruffians made me feel seriously put upon. Especially as I was carefully carrying a paper-wrapped and twine-bound package containing the fine new garments and boots I had acquired through the courtesy of Mr. Abraham ben Zaccheus's generosity and good will.

Can you imagine the embarrassment I would have felt if I had lost my package and had to return to Mr. Abraham ben Zaccheus's establishment penniless and empty-handed? This good gentleman had taken me in and treated me with such kindness, I would have been mortally ashamed to do such a thing.

Well, one of the toughs was facing me. The street was not brightly lit, but I could see the villain fairly well, courtesy of some moonlight and a bit of illumination coming from the music hall I had just left. This worthy was wearing a sailor's pea-jacket and watch-cap and sported a nifty set of brass knuckles combined with a polished belly-ripper on one hand. That hand looked pretty small and slim, so slim it made me suspect I was facing a woman.

And when the ruffian spoke I decided that I was right. This was indeed a female bandit.

A scandal, thought I.

She said something which I could not comprehend, as it was in a heathenish language with which I was unfamiliar. I could not tell if she was speaking to me or to someone standing behind me. I think she spoke a name, something like *Zany*, and since I couldn't understand her I thought indeed that she was speaking to someone else.

And sure enough there was a second voice, a nasty-sounding man's voice, speaking practically in my ear. I think this fellow called the woman a villain, or some such thing.

The woman gestured with her knuckles-and-belly-ripper. I imagine that she was expecting me to back away from her. But someone — and one of the Holy Saints,

I'm sure — seemed to be whispering in my ear, *John O'Leary, don't you do that!*

Instead of backing away, I shoved my brown paper bundle straight at the woman's face, at the same moment dodging to one side and dropping to one knee.

Glory be to that whispering Saint! I wish I knew which one it was.

The tough with the knuckles-and-blade on her hand had a confederate, as I've already indicated. Said confederate, as I shortly learned, was dressed similarly to the first villain, but instead of brass knuckles and blade he was armed with a ship's belaying pin which he was in the process of bringing down upon my own dear unprotected bazoo, the which I value highly and have done my level best to protect ever since I was a wee tyke lacking both hair and choppers.

Oh, it was a lovely sight I then beheld.

The female ruffian with the knuckles-and-blade found her weapon embedded in my package. The fellow with the belaying pin in his hand was already in the act of delivering his mightiest wallop, upon which landed squarely, but not on my own precious crown but that of his partner.

They fell to scuffling angrily, rolling on the cobblestones, growling and snapping and biting like a pair of mongrel hounds, and I could give my warrant that the female scoundrel, though far the smaller of the two, was likely to get the best of the fight. I could have sworn that she was going for her partner's jugular with her teeth, yes, like some creature out of a novel by the great Mr. Stoker.

While they went at it I retrieved my package, the brass weapon still attached to it, and made tracks as fast as my lower limbs would carry me.

A sight I must have been when I rapped once again at the door of Mr. Abraham ben Zaccheus's house on Rooshian Hill, what with my phiz all perspired and my locks in disarray. But Mr. Abraham ben Zaccheus ushered me for the second time into his home, bolting the door behind me.

I feared that my appearance might cost me my new position, and not only that, would leave me indebted in the amount of two silver dollars to my employer, but when once I had recounted my adventure of the evening such was not the result. In fact, as I narrated the past hours' events, which I did with complete accuracy and with no embellishment whatsoever, Abraham guffawed repeatedly.

This set to rest another falsehood that I had been told by the Father in Kilkee. His teaching it was that Hebrews are unable to laugh like other men, but only to emit a gleeful cackle at the misfortune of their foes, which is to say, all good and faithful followers of Our Lord. Instead, Mr. Abraham ben Zaccheus laughed heartily at the image of the two ruffians rolling around in the gutter as I made off safe and sound with my bundle, the knuckles-and-blade device still attached thereto.

Abraham drew a huge bandanna from his pocket, wiped his streaming eyes, and blew his large nose loudly. On that score, at least, the Father was correct. Abraham's nose was truly majestic. When he had regained his breath he asked to examine the weapon I had liberated from my attackers.

He turned it over in his hands, tested the edge of the blade against his thumb, and returned it to my custody. Quoth he: 'A good thing that you kept the weapon, John. Take care of it. We may find it useful.' He then offered me a nightcap of a beverage he called *schnapps*, which I found most tasty and enjoyable, and in which he raised a toast in a language unknown to me.

Abraham did ask me to repeat the conversation the two toughs had held, both before attacking me and during their scuffle. I scratched my head to help me recall their heathenish words, then recounted them as best I could.

'You had a narrow escape, young John,' Abraham said when I was finished. I studied his phiz trying to cipher his age but with not great success. Surely he was older than my own years, but I thought not by so much as to call me young. But he was the employer, you see, and I the worker, and it was not for me to challenge him on this score.

It was not as if I was back in Kilkee and he was the Father!

'Your attackers,' Abraham told me, 'were almost certainly Zanna and Veleno. They are two of the most dangerous street-prowlers in this city. Obviously, you did not get a good look at Zanna's face, or you would have mentioned it. She is by all reports one of the most beautiful women alive. I have encountered her before, and I can affirm that those reports are neither falsehoods nor exaggerations. As for her consort, Veleno, he is reputed to have killed no fewer than an hundred men in his native Sicily, and half again as many in America.'

He paused to inhale deeply. Then he said, 'You were fortunate to get away unscathed, but you not only escaped those two, you humiliated them. I am afraid, John O'Leary, that you have made two very dangerous enemies.'

Abraham sighed, patted me upon the knee, and said, 'There is nothing more to do this night save get a good rest. A busy day awaits us tomorrow.'

And so we retired for the night, he to

whatever quarters he chose to use, it being his house, and I to a comfortable room which Abraham assigned me.

In the morning we shared a hearty breakfast served by his housekeeper. Abraham's 'Mrs. Hudson' was a lady of the Chinese persuasion, whose name I later learned was rendered *Xiang Xu-Mei*, meaning fragrant beautiful plum. Xiang Xu-Mei was a most pleasant person and a talented chef. She fluttered around her employer, patting him and speaking to him in her native tongue, the which, to my astonishment, Mr. Abraham ben Zaccheus must have understood, for he replied in the same language.

Next, Abraham told me we were to explore the site of his pending investigation. Refreshed and nourished, we made our way to an elegant carriage house, which stood on the grounds behind Abraham's home. He swung open the door to reveal, not the horse and buggy which I had begun to anticipate, but an odd looking contrivance of metal and wood and cloth.

The horseless carriage had yet to make

its way to the village of Kilkee. Horse-drawn buggies and dog-carts serve the needs of them as can afford them. When the mighty Bishop Quigley himself arrived one time for a pastoral visit riding regally inside a steam automobile, the conveyance rather than the Right Reverend Lordship was the focus of all eyes and the topic of conversation at the pub for days to come. It was raining that day, and His Reverend Lordship stayed high and dry inside the carriage while some poor baby priest, he looked to be fresh from the seminary, sat outside in a sopping-wet cassock, driving the contrivance.

My good friend Seamus McCarthy, he was a fellow of a scientific bent, mind you, Seamus McCarthy speculated on that steam carriage. 'If the boiler blows,' Seamus asked, 'I suppose his Grand Holiness in there would be all right, but that poor sap of a youngster riding on top would be cooked for sure and blown to bits. We'd find chunks of sanctified stew meat strewing the countryside for a fortnight, I should think.'

You might infer by now that Kilkee was not the most pious of towns, and you'd not be far wrong at that.

Indeed, I saw plenty of horseless carriages in Dublin and Liverpool and the great cities of this great land America, but I must confess that I never rode in one until Mr. Abraham ben Zaccheus directed me to climb aboard his vehicle, and he sat right there in it beside me. It didn't look nor feel so different from a lovely buggy, and he was proud as punch of the conveyance.

'A Columbia Mark LX Runabout,' he told me, grinning like a new dad showing off a fresh-hatched chick. I bought it at the factory and drove it across the continent myself.'

I found that hard to believe, but I was not inclined to challenge the veracity of my employer, you can be sure.

He started up the machine and slid the controller handle a notch to roll it forward, informing me that the estimable Xiang Xiu-mei would see to closing up the carriage house after we were gone. We started off down Rooshian Hill, and I will admit that I was frightened for my very life and hung on as tightly as I could while the machine rolled down the sloping way.

'Did you sleep well, John?' he asked me.

'Well indeed,' I told him. It took all of my powers to hold a conversation while clutching at the buggy-railing.

'And you felt nothing, nor noticed an unpleasant odor in the night?'

'I did awaken once,' I conceded. 'I thought perhaps I'd been dreaming, that my bed was moving about, or perhaps the whole house.'

'What else?'

'Mayhap I smelt something, Abraham. I couldn't tell for certain. I thought perhaps it was the Coleraine thirty-four in my belly complaining about the Glenmorangie I sipped on top of it. You know, the finest Irish and that pissy-poor stuff the Scots call whiskey, you should pardon my French if you will, Abraham, they don't really get along so well.'

'Mayhap,' Abraham said, and that was all he said just then.

We had reached the bottom of Rooshian Hill and were navigating the streets of San Francisco. The clouds and misty drizzle of yesterday had blown away and the sun was shining. The streets of this city were crowded with a variety of folk, some men and women in finery such as you'd find in the best cities in the world and some in rough worker's garb or worse. There were rumpots falling down in the gutter and there were ruined souls with the mark of the Chinese hop on their faces.

You could hear every language in the world spoken in those streets, and a kind of street railway pulled by underground cables ran on some thoroughfares while horse cars ran on others and wagons and buggies of every description battled for headroom.

At last we reached a section of the city where new buildings were rising at every turn. On Turk Street, Abraham drew up in front of a spanking new building four stories tall. He climbed from his electric buggy, inviting me to do the same, the which I did. He stood looking up at the edifice before us. It was built all of cut stones, as solid and gloomy as a cathedral. There were tall windows of colored glass and patterns that might have meant something if they hadn't been so murky and shifty-looking, like castor oil dropped in a pan of water. There was a weathervane, I think, on the roof. It was hard to tell just what it was meant to represent. Maybe a rooster.

Abraham was wearing what the Frenchies call a sacque suit all of black, a shirt the color of a ripe plum, a four-in-hand cravat and a bowler hat over his biretta thing, which he told me Hebrews call a *yarmee-kee*. He had brought one of those new electric torches with him in his horseless carriage. Oh, he was an electric man, was Abraham ben Zaccheus. He cut a noteworthy figure altogether but I felt comfortable in my new denims and boots with a knitted watch cap to keep my ears warm.

One odd thing about this city, it doesn't have a climate. You can travel a mile in any direction and go from sunshine to fog, warm air to chill wind.

The weather had been as pleasant as a bright morn in early springtime up there on Rooshian Hill. Here on Turk Street the sky had turned a dull gray and the wind blew specks of grit in my face.

Abraham placed his hand on my forearm. He had a heavy hand, not the soft thing that you'd expect a bookish fellow to have, no less gentleman of royal birth, for I was still not settled in my own mind as to who Abraham ben Zaccheus really was. He wore a heavy gold ring that looked as if it had once been a living thing that had somehow crawled onto his finger and liked the climate so much it decided to stay. I couldn't tell whether it had eyes or tiny jewels for eyes, but surely it was looking at me even as I was looking at it, and I will confess that I was the first one to look away.

'What do you feel, John?' Abraham asked me.

'Only your hand on my arm, sir.'

He shook his head. 'Nothing from — ' He tilted his head toward the ground beneath our feet.

'Nothing, sir.'

He let out a sigh and shook his head. 'All right, John, all right. How about the air? Do you smell anything?'

I took a sniff. Indeed, I smelled a great many things. I could smell the Pacific Ocean with all of the life and all of the death that goes on in its waters, from California to Cathay. I could smell the grass and palm trees in Mr. McLaren's great Golden Gate Park. I'll give him credit for that, Scotsman though he is. I could smell the shishkee-bobs that street vendors were making over little charcoal fires. And I could smell the droppings of the horses that pulled carriages and drays through the city's streets.

But when I told Abraham what I could smell, he was clearly disappointed. 'Don't you smell something else, John O'Leary? Don't you smell something evil?'

'No,' I shook my head.

Abraham muttered into his beard, then he looked up into my face and fixed me with his great dark eyes. 'We're going into that building,' he said, 'and you must be on your guard. I may need your help. My life will be in your hands, John O'Leary.'

35

He took his hand off my arm and grasped me by the wrists. 'In your hands,' he said again. There was a serious expression on his face, one I hadn't seen before. 'When we are in the building I want you to hold your tongue, John. Do not speak to anyone you meet there, no matter who you may think they are, nor what they may say to you. Listen only to me. If you hear me say the word *ayin*, you are to act as if you remembered something very urgent and important and insist that we leave at once.'

I didn't know what to make of that, and I suppose I looked a bit puzzled, but then Abraham did something that surprised me. He reached up and grabbed me by the ears, and brought my face down so close to his that I could count the hairs in his dark beard, and he said, 'John, our hosts may try to keep us there. I may try to stay, myself. I may tell you that I've changed my mind, that you can leave but that I need to stay behind. You are to ignore everything that happens, everything that I say, everything that anyone says. If you hear the word I've given you,

you must get me out of there. Do you understand me, John?'

I said I did.

'And what is the word?' he asked.

I said, 'Ayin.'

He let go of my head and I straightened up. 'Good. Very good. You are a fine fellow, John O'Leary, a very fine fellow. Now remember what I told you. And repeat the word to me once more.'

I said, 'Ayin.'

'Good.'

'Abraham,' I said, 'what does it mean? Ayin, what does it mean?'

He said, 'Nothing. Just remember it, and remember what you are to do if you hear me speak it.'

We made our way to the house, Abraham taking short strides as befits a man of his height and build, and I taking longer ones as befits a man such as myself. We climbed a stoop and Abraham nodded to me, indicating that I should knock on the door, which I would have done with my knuckles had there not been a splendid brass knocker attached to the wood. It looked something like a sea creature, and I wondered if the house was not the new home of a seagoing trader.

The door let into a darkened anteroom, the likes of which I believe the Frenchies call a *four-yea*, and we stepped inside.

I will confess that my jaw dropped, for where should I find myself but the vestibule of St. Padraic's Church. The doors to the nave were wide open, and there was Father Phinean himself, a greasy, frayed dog collar visible over his chasuble. He smiled at me and reached his hand to me. I thought he was going to give me another clout and I think I raised my own paw to protect my cauliflower ear, but he took my other hand in his and shook it.

His skin was cold.

He said something to me. At first I couldn't tell what he was saying, it was in some language I'd never encountered before, but then I could understand. He was saying, *Welcome, my son, welcome, we haven't seen you at St. Padraic's in a long time, young John. You've come to make Confession, I hope. I know you've sinned, young John.*

Past him I could see the chancel, and above it a clerestory where, glory be, the choir was practicing their parts of the Mass. At least, I thought that was what they were practicing. They weren't singing in Latin and the tune was not what I thought they should be singing.

Come along, Father Phinean said. He put his arm around my shoulders and it felt strange to me, strong as an ox and yet I couldn't tell where his elbow or his wrist were, his arm was all like a single giant muscle inside his skin. *Come along*.

He drew me toward the chancel. He came to the altar and knelt, acting like a proper priest, and made some gesture that I couldn't see but it should have been the Sign of the Cross. I knelt, too, and when Father Phinean stood up again I did the same and then I turned around to see if Abraham ben Zaccheus was still with us but he was nowhere to be seen.

Instead I beheld none other than his high and mighty lordship Bishop Quigley himself, as splendid as he could be in his stole and alb and all the rest of his royal robes, wearing a miter on his head like a crown and holding a crozier in his hand like a royal scepter. The baby priest who had attended him so long ago in Kilkee stood at his side to render help should he be needed.

For all that I was fallen away from the Church I went to my knees and bowed my head before the mighty Bishop and he held out his hand to me. I saw he was wearing a ring. I thought none less than the Holy Father Himself would wear such a ring but Bishop Quigley was wearing one. It was gold and had a sigil all worked into it. I raised it to my lips and felt a jolt go through me like the Holy Spirit Himself, or maybe a wallop of the electricity Abraham ben Zaccheus seemed so fond of.

The Bishop made me stand up.

The choir were singing.

Father Phinean said, *Come along, then, young John O'Leary*.

There was a trap door behind the altar. The Lord Bishop's baby priest opened it and we proceeded down stone steps into the Earth beneath St. Padraic's, first portly Bishop Quigley then tall Father

Phinean and then myself, wondering and wide-eyed, smelling the incense of my youth and dreaming up the image of dear Maeve Corrigan with her red hair and green eyes and pale, soft skin.

We tramped down and down. The Bishop was huffing and puffing as he went along, leaning on his crozier. I could feel a hand on my shoulder, and thought that it was the baby priest, Bishop Quigley's driver and man-of-all-tasks. There were walls around us, roughly hewn from bedrock, with carvings lit by cressets that must burn oil, and there was the smell of incense, and there was a rumbling from below as if some great machinery was working away in the bowels of the Earth.

The bowels of the Earth beneath Kilkee.

And singing. Singing. The choir was far above us, practicing away in the clerestory, but there was new singing from below us, from wherever the stone stairs led.

At last we found ourselves in an open area like none I had seen in all my days. I blinked and blinked and tried to tell what it was I beheld, but I could not. Mayhap we were in a natural cavern deep in Mother Earth's dear womb, or mayhap we were out-of-doors in the night, for I thought I beheld stars and planets, swooping comets and distant galaxies, our own Milky Way as I'd seen on many nights looking at the sky above Kilkee and other bodies of stars, great swirling masses and whole universes twisting and writhing like starfish fresh drawn from the briny ocean. There was every color I knew and there were colors I had never imagined could exist.

We walked and there was a pit, and in it great beasts that slithered and wove like worms in a fisherman's bucket only a thousand, a million times the size. It was their pounding and squirming that had made the great thumping and grinding sounds.

But there rose up from the pit a crowd of boys and girls. The great beasts had disappeared and there was a green field and there was a picnic going on. There was Malachy Teague and there was

42

Seamus McCarthy, there was Rogan Doherty and Shane Galloway, and Glenna Lynch, little Glenna Lynch, her hair done up in pigtails.

And there was Maeve Corrigan, Maeve Corrigan alive and flaunting her flaming locks at me, giving me a come-on glance from her green eyes, innocent and eager all at once, and she raised her white as snow hand and gestured to me. It felt as though she touched me. I started forward, started toward my friends Shane and Rogan, Seamus and Malachy, little Glenna and beautiful my love my Maeve.

But up steps Bishop Quigley, shouting at me in some language I've never heard before, saying words I dast not repeat save I heard among them *Ayin, Ayin, Ayin*, meaning, Abraham ben Zaccheus had told me, means nothing. He had his miter on his poll and crozier raised in two hands like a jousting pole and he swings the crozier and smites me in the belly and I blink and Maeve is gone, little Glenna and my Shane and Rogan and Seamus and Malachy are gone and the great beasts are back, with their many heads

43

and their ropy arms and their stench, O God, their stench.

And Father Phinean isn't Father Phinean either, he's one of the beasts only smaller, and the baby priest, Bishop Quigley's man, is another.

And Bishop Quigley, his crozier is the new electric torch that Abraham ben Zaccheus carried with him this day, and his miter is King Abraham's *yarmee kee* hat, and his vestments are King Abraham's black sacque suit. And Bishop Quigley is none other than King Abraham ben Zaccheus.

The not-Father Phinean and the not-baby priest come roaring at King Abraham and at me, shouting words of their own in some language I didn't know, and I rear up, I feel the rage in me, the fury I never knew was even in me, and I take them one in each hand by the neck and I squeeze. They are covered with slime and filth that burns my hands and stinks in my nostrils and makes me gag like rotten food only ten times ten times worse.

With one beast in each hand I lift them

from the ground and raise them into the air, into the air that stinks of incense gone to evil, and I toss them like two rotting, stinking dead conies that have lain in the field for a month into the pit where the great horrid beasts open mouths on red horrid throats and close those mouths midst gnashing of teeth and screaming, and swallow them like two delicious morsels.

Abraham ben Zaccheus and I started up the stone steps that had led us down to that evil place. We climbed and climbed. Soon Abraham was huffing and puffing but I kept him going, up and up until we were back in the chancel. We stumbled past the altar and up the nave. Abraham stopped and leaned on me, gasping until he regained some breath and some composure.

The stained glass windows above us showed scenes like the galaxies in the Kilkee sky.

We made our way to the great wooden doors.

Beneath us the rumbling grew louder and the very church began to shake. We stumbled out and paused to slam the doors shut behind us. Would we find ourselves in Kilkee, I wondered, or back on Turk Street in the City of San Francisco?

St. Padraic's church shook visibly on its foundation.

The weathervane rising from its roof toppled and fell with a crash. I saw that it was a starfish kind of thing that seemed almost to be alive, as big across as a calf, lying writhing at our feet.

The stained glass windows shattered with a sound like an explosion and flames and smoke rose from the building. The very Earth shook. There was a stench like the stench I had smelled inside the church, but so powerful that it nearly stole my consciousness from me.

A host of rats came pouring from the building, and I could have sworn that among them were some forms more human than rat. Did I see my acquaintances of the alley, the beautiful Zanna and the nasty Veleno? I couldn't tell, for in a moment they were gone, the rats were gone, and there was nothing to show that they had been there.

Men and women came running to see what was happening, and in a bit I heard the clatter of hoofs and the gongs and horns of a fire company.

Abraham ben Zaccheus grabbed my arm and hustled me into his electric carriage. He moved the lever and we glided silently along Turk Street, passing men and women running to see what was taking place.

An hour later we were in Abraham's house on Rooshian Hill. Abraham had washed himself clean of the filth and the stink of the house on Turk Street, and donned a fresh outfit. I had done the same.

We sat in Abraham's parlor. Xiang Xu-Mai, the fragrant beautiful plum, had brought us both warm broth and biscuits and I found that I had a goodly appetite, as had Abraham.

'That evil place is gone,' Abraham said, lowering his spoon and wiping his lips on a square of linen.

'Is there no more menace, then?' I asked him.

He ignored my question and instead placed one of his own. 'John O'Leary, what did you see?'

'I saw Bishop Quigley and his baby priest helper, and Father Phinean,' I told him. 'I saw my old church in Kilkee.' I stopped, a bit of biscuit caught in throat, or something, for I could not speak,

'It's all right, John.' Abraham nodded kindly to me. The pictures of his ancestors and his Emperor gazed down upon us from the walls of his parlor. 'Speak when you can. Is that all you saw?'

'No,' I said. 'I saw my friends, Your Majesty. I saw Rogan and Malachy and little Glenna.' Another bit of biscuit caught in my throat and brought tears to my eyes. 'And my dear Maeve, Abraham, my Maeve was there.'

'She was not,' he said. 'I'm sorry. What you saw was not what was there.'

I fixed him with a glare. 'Then you did not see Rogan or Malachy or Maeve? You did not see Bishop Quigley or Father Phinean?'

'No.' He shook his head.

'What did you see? What did you see,

Your Majesty?' I asked.

'No.' He shook his head. He was wearing his little biretta thing, his *yarmee kee* hat and a fresh sacque suit and his spade-shaped beard that I thought was all black, I realized, had a few little streaks of gray in it.

'Ayin,' he said. 'Ayin.'

There Are Kings

Indeed, indeed there are kings. There are kings all over the world, you know. Some of them wear crowns and ermine robes, they sit on thrones and hold scepters when they're at home in their palaces and when they travel about they ride in golden coaches.

I've seen pictures, indeed.

They sit in their palaces in Spain and Prussia and Rome and Rooshia. There's the king of the Ottoman Empire, they call him a Sultan, and in India they call them Rogers and they have an emperor in China and another one in Japan. Oh, yes. I've seen pictures.

And there's Edward Saxe-Coburg-Gotha the German libertine King of England sitting there in London and pretending to be King of Ireland. Let him think what he likes, the villain. Ireland has a king of her own, don't you worry, and his time will come. Mayhap I'll live to see an Irish king ruling from Dublin and mayhap I'll be in my grave when he comes, but I have no doubt that he lives somewhere, and when the stars are right he will claim his throne and the Germans will haul their fat selves back to England where they belong.

I don't know why the English want a German king anyway, but that's their business. It is the Irish whose wants I care for, and the Irish want an Irish king!

Now Mr. Abraham ben Zaccheus, he's another tale altogether. I give him the courtesy of calling him Mister because that's his preference, but in my heart I know he's a king. Mayhap he's His Imperial and Apostolic Majesty, by the Grace of God, Emperor of Austria, King of Hungary and Bohemia, and a lot of other things, too, that he denies he is. I know that he is a Hebrew, and I know that Our Lord and Savior was the King of the Jews, by which I know is meant the Hebrews, and this gives me to wonder if King Abraham is not the King of the Jews in this, the blessed Twentieth Century, and he chooses to humble himself by pretending to be a plain Mister instead of an Imperial and Apostolic Majesty.

I would really not know.

But he says to me the other night not long after dinner, 'John O'Leary,' he says, 'John O'Leary, are you ready to take a little trip on the morrow?'

This is his way, is Abraham ben Zaccheus's way. If he is a king he would simply command, would he not, and even if he is the plain citizen that he pretends to be, he is still my employer. He gives me room and board in his fine little house upon Rooshian Hill and he pays me a handsome salary each week in silver and gold. He could simply say, 'John, get yourself ready to leave in the morning,' but that is not his way.

So I says, 'At your service, Your Majesty,' and he says, 'Stop that, please, just call me Abraham,' and I says, 'Whatever Your Majesty commands, Abraham.'

And I wink at my employer and he winks at me.

We're sitting in his comfortable parlor. Abraham, a wider man than I and sporting as he does a spade-shaped beard and a comfortable corporation beneath his vest, is settled upon the horsehair couch. I, a taller man than he and somewhat narrower in the fundament, am at home in the easy chair. Between us on the polished low table is a bottle of fine dry sherry and a plate of sponge-cake, the latter baked by Abraham's housekeeper Xiang Xu-Mei, a plump and pleasant lady of the Chinee persuasion.

For reasons of his own, I am sure good and sufficient reasons, Abraham chose not to speak of where I was to go in the morning, nor of whether I was to proceed on my lonesome or with company. Instead, he delivered himself of a disquisition on the subject of gods and demons, of priests and saints, some of which I understood and some of which I did not, all punctuated by regular refilling of our glasses from the golden store.

When the great clock that stood against the red-flocked wall of Abraham's sitting room struck one he blinked and said to me, 'John, I've talked too long and said too little. We need our rest. Get to your room and I shall get to mine, and we assemble for an early breakfast if you please.'

As I got to my feet he added, 'Dress warmly in the morning, John O'Leary.'

And I said I would, as if one would dress any other way in the first days of January in this fine city of San Francisco.

I retired and slept the sleep of the somewhat innocent, in my dreams returning to Kilkee as I often do, to my friends Shane Galloway and Rogan Doherty and Seamus McCarthy and Malachy Teague, to Glenna Lynch who taught me a thing or two about her gender and to Maeve Corrigan whom I loved dearly until an Englishman's horse kicked her in the head and we buried her behind St. Padraic's Church so long ago.

And in the morning King Abraham's housekeeper the estimable Xiang Xu-Mei was ready for us with coffee and juice and eggs and sourdough bread toasted atop the woodstove. Abraham pulled a time-piece from the belly pocket of his vest and after consulting it said, 'We'd best make haste, John, we've a long journey ahead of us this day.'

Xiang Xu-Mei had packed a carpetbag for Abraham and a valise for myself. They stood beside the door and as we exited the house Abraham exchanged a few words with the housekeeper in her own tongue, which talent never ceases to amaze me. Many a hint has Abraham dropped into our chats about the places he has visited, be they the steppes of Rooshia or the high town of Lhasa in distant Tibet, but how old he is and how many lands he has seen I cannot tell you.

It was a journey indeed, by Mr. Halliday's wondrous cable car to the pier, by ferry to the fine town of Oak-Land, and thence by the Central Pacific Railroad's comfortable service eastward.

Abraham was not inclined to converse as our train made its way through delta and farmland. I whiled away the time reading one of the fine novels of Mr. William Westall, which I had procured at a shop on Taylor Street in San Francisco. It was *The Phantom City, a Volcanic Romance*, and it served well to while away the hours. At the same time Abraham occupied himself with a heavy volume he had brought from his own library. I would tell you its name but it was one of those odd books the writing of which was in some alphabet we never learned in Kilkee. I think Abraham might have brought that book back from one of his adventures, written by some ancient hand long ago in the mountains of Tibet or in some pillared city in Araby.

After passing the city of Sacramento where Governor Henry Gage reigns in splendor, our train began its climb through the wondrous Sierras, a range of mountains as beautiful as any in the world. As we rose toward the town of Auburn the graceful pines that covered the slopes began to show signs of the winter's snows.

The Central Pacific furnishes its trains with dining cars where they serve as fine a cuisine as any restaurant. I found myself wondering if the estimable Xiang Xu-Mei had packed sandwiches for Abraham and myself, but to my great pleasure Abraham suggested that we hie ourselves to the dining car, where we put away a delightful repast of fresh trout and tiny potatoes, accompanied by an adequate bottle of local origin.

Night was falling when we debarked at the town of Truckee. A porter transferred Abraham's carpet bag and my valise to the care of the Lake Tahoe Railway and Transportation Company, and after a shorter and less comfortable train ride we found ourselves transferring yet again, to a horse-drawn station wagon that carried us to the Tahoe Tavern. Ah, a lovely establishment that was, as if a giant had ordered built a rustic cabin for himself, only to change his mind and command that it be furnished with the luxury of a grand hotel.

Aye, and Abraham and I found ourselves shortly escorted to the great dining room of the establishment. Formally clad waiters took our order, and elegantly gowned ladies and nicely tailored gentlemen sat at tables surrounding ours. Imagine, imagine, a Hebrew and an Irishman dining off white linen and transparent china, surrounded by such aristocracy. This America is a wondrous land! The repast was splendid, a fillet of local piscines accompanied by a good wine, followed by a tasty nightcap in the saloon.

At one point during the meal I had discovered two ladies seated without companions at a nearby table watching Abraham and myself. They were gowned and hatted as would befit persons of quality, and I detected the younger of the two sending an appraising glance my way. I responded with a merry wink, and was rewarded with a charming blush.

Ah, there is no sight more charming than that of a lady in pleased repose, her hair on her pillow, spread about her face like a saint's halo in a stained glass window.

Later I lay abed, the curtains pulled back and the night sky showing an array of splendor such as I could recall never having seen in my life. The stars were brilliant, the Milky Way seemed to flow across the heavens like a river of lights, and the reflected light of the moon as it peered just over the peak of a snow-covered mountain turning the snow-covered surrounding lawns and woods into an artist's dream.

It was a sheer startlement to me when I felt my shoulder grasped by a strong hand. I had not realized that I had fallen asleep, but I looked up and recognized King Abraham leaning over me, his finger pressed to his lips to indicate the need for silence. I blinked and sat up, rubbing the slumber from my eyes. I whispered, 'What is it, Abraham? What time is it?'

'Time for us to be about our work, John O'Leary. Climb into your warmest clothing, and be quick, please.'

In minutes we were outside the Tahoe Tavern. The moon had risen higher into the sky and its brilliant light reflecting off a fresh fall of snow made the world as bright as day, but a day to which the white earth and the black sky with its twinkling stars and glaring moon lent a weird unreality.

Once we were out of earshot of the Tavern, Abraham halted and fixed me with an earnest look. His eyes seemed larger and darker than ever I had seen them. 'You've been a patient man, John O'Leary. You've surely wondered why we are here.'

'Indeed I have, Your Majesty.'

A hint of a suggestion of a grin whipped across his face but he made no mention of my addressing him by a title of royalty.

He said, 'We've a walk ahead of us. I'll tell you something of our purpose here as we proceed.'

He was a man of his word, was Abraham ben Zaccheus. We were both equipped with heavy boots. I wore two layers of warm stocking beneath my own, and I should have thought Abraham was similarly attired in the pedal department. We both wore heavy gloves and warm hats. The air was cold but so clean and dry after the night's snowfall that it provided great stimulation and refreshment.

'There is a Chinee village not far from here,' Abraham told me. 'The Chinee arrived as laborers, imported to work on the railroads in California. But the workers were all male, and the authorities chose to exclude their women so as to prevent our state from being overwhelmed by a horde of yellow barbarians.'

'I did not know that.'

'Few do. And a small number of Chinee women have found one way or another to enter California. My housekeeper, Xiang Xu-Mei, is one such. There are now thriving Chinee communities in this state. These people will not die.'

We passed beneath a tall tree at this point. A soft breeze swept snow off its branches and needles, and Abraham and I found ourselves beneath a new snowfall. We continued walking. Abraham continued his explanation.

'The village of which I spoke, however, remained entirely male. With the passing years some of its members have left for other communities. Those who stayed behind grew old and one by one went to their rewards. In due course there were only two men left in the village. They were brothers. One was a Buddhist priest. The other had been a chef and he continued to cook for the two of them. One of them was one hundred four years old; the other, one hundred two. Neither knew which was the older. Each insisted that it was he.'

We had emerged from beneath a stand of fir trees and halted on a snow-covered slope. Ahead I saw a pitiable collection of wooden shanties. Smoke arose from a stove-pipe that poked through a thin layer of snow atop one of them, a ramshackle structure that looked little more than a shed.

'A few days ago, one of the brothers died. The one who had cooked for them. I was summoned by the surviving brother. I asked you to accompany me, John O'Leary, for I need your support. You are strong, you have courage and your heart is pure.'

'Abraham,' I confessed, 'I'm not above a dalliance now and then, and I've put my fist through the belly of many a rascal.'

He ignored my words, so I took my courage in hand and asked, 'How were you summoned, Abraham?'

To this he only shook his head. He crooked his finger at me as best he could through the thick glove that covered his hand. We tramped onward through the fresh snow. The great dark lake loomed at the bottom of the slope.

When we reached the hut with the stove-pipe Abraham knocked on the door and spoke briefly in the language I recognized, now, from his conversations with Xiang Xu-Mei. The response from inside was a murmur so low that I was not sure I heard it at all. Abraham lowered his head and mumbled a few more words that I did not understand. He pushed the door open and stepped into the hut.

I followed him.

An iron stove must have warmed the hut somewhat, but I felt no less cold inside than I had outside. I shoved the door to, behind me. Embers glowed in the stove; through openings in its door they cast flickering light into the room.

Sitting cross-legged facing the stove was the oldest man I had ever clapped eyes on. His head was bare and his skull was shaved. He wore a long scraggly beard. He was wrapped in a robe that looked like the toga Julius Caesar himself wore in the history book Father Phinean taught us from back in Kilkee.

The old man's eyes were open and bright with life and with the reflected glare of the embers. He smiled ever so slightly at Abraham, then sighed and closed his eyes and his soul was gone. Gone to wherever souls go. Ah, if I'd expressed that doubt back in Kilkee, Father Phinean would have clouted me for it, but here in America one is free to think what he thinks and to ask what he asks, is he not?

King Abraham leaned over the old man and drew his eyelids down over his eyes. Then he leaned farther and pressed his lips to the cold brow of the dead priest. He straightened, then, and nodded solemnly, and said, 'This is why we are here, John O'Leary.'

'To bury this man?' I asked.

'No. Others will tend to that, and the body matters not in any case, John. You've much to learn.'

Oh, I knew that. He was telling me nothing new.

'This is very bad. This is why we are here.'

So saying, His Imperial and Apostolic Majesty King Abraham indicated a thing that the old man had held in his two hands. Even in death he held it, nor did Abraham ben Zaccheus touch it at that moment.

It was a statue, some seven or eight inches high. It seemed made of stone, but so cunningly done that it could have been a real, living thing. In the red glow of the embers from the old man's stove, its color might have been purple or blue or gray, I could not tell.

I moved my hand toward it but to my great surprise Abraham struck me aside. He had never struck me before and I stood waiting for him to explain.

'For the good of your soul, John, do not touch that thing. Your thick gloves may offer some small protection, but you would regret for all your days if you touched it.'

'But the old man is holding it,' I replied.

'The old man studied for a hundred years, John. He could work wonders that even I could only marvel at. He could handle the statue, but you dare not, believe me.'

He looked around the inside of the hut until he found an old wooden box that must once have held raw victuals. He placed the box beneath the statue and carefully pried the old man's hands apart. With a dull thud the statue fell into the box. Abraham drew a bandanna from a pocket of his heavy coat and covered the statue. Then he rose to his feet and proceeded toward the door. He held the wooden box in both his arms. I leaped ahead and cleared the way for him.

We walked from the hut, from the Chinee village, now left without a single inhabitant. At length Abraham halted and knelt in the snow. He laid the box on the cold snow. He uncovered the statue. Now, in the glare of the full moon, I could see it properly, and wish I had not. It was the foulest, evilest thing I have ever beheld. It looked a little like a man, but its head was something like that of a squid like they sell on the wharfs in San Francisco. It face was horrid to behold, a mass of feelers, and its body was all scaly and rubbery looking. It had arms and legs something like a man's but more like a frog's, with prodigious claws on its fingers and toes. Its shoulders sprouted long, narrow wings that it might have used to fly through the air like a bat or through the sea like a devil-ray. It squatted on a rectangular block or pedestal covered with characters in some script that no human mind had ever imagined.

'Now, John O'Leary,' Abraham said to me, 'now you know. Now you know what evil truly is.' He covered the statue once more. He stood then, and told me to take the box but not to touch the statue itself.

We had cast our shadows in the moonlight, so dark against the pale snow that they seemed almost blue. But there was a crack from behind us and the snow around our shadows became suddenly orange. I turned and saw that the old man's hut had burst into flames. As Abraham and I watched, the conflagration spread to the other shacks in the Chinee village, and in the wink of an eye the village was no more.

'As well,' Abraham said. 'It's as well.

Come now, our night's work is just beginning.'

He led me through more stands of trees and more snow-covered hillsides until I had no idea where I was, save that the moon remained a bright lantern among the stars and the lake a dark presence. I wondered that it was not frozen in this cold winter, but there was no white on its face except for the reflection of the moon. I was inclined to ask Abraham where we were going but a single look at his face, his great dark eyes and spade-shaped beard streaked with white, told me that I would receive no answer and that it were best to hold my tongue.

At length Abraham halted and laid a thick-gloved hand on my elbow. With his other hand he pointed to still another village. This one was made of Indian tents. I'd seen others on the Great Plains on my way to California, but this was the closest I had ever been to them. The camp looked newer and more prosperous than the dying Chinee village that now smoldered far behind us on the snowy hillside.

'The Washoes.'

I asked what he meant.

'The Washoes,' he repeated. 'They lived here before the white man came. They named the lake, although the white man's name for it, Tahoe, is a corruption of the Washoe name.'

He nodded toward the village and said, 'Stay with me but do not put down your burden, and do not let the covering come from off the statue.'

Ah, I was not so happy to hold onto that statue, but I was more than happy to leave it covered by Abraham's bandanna.

Abraham went to the largest tent in the camp. He motioned me to stay outside while he went inside and conferred. I heard his voice, and others, but the language was a new one to me. Surely it was not Chinee.

After a time Abraham came back out of the tent. A tall fellow followed him, his hair long and black, his face like a hawk's. He ignored me. He went to a couple of other tents and got a man out of each. He had to be a chief, that was clear. You see, there are kings everywhere. On Rooshian

Hill, Abraham was king. Here, the chief was king. I know I said that Indian kings are called Rogers, but this was a different kind of Indian. These kings are called chiefs.

The chief spoke to his men in their language, and then Abraham spoke to them some more in their language, and then we set off down the hillside, through the snow, toward the black lake. I carried the box with that statue in it. For a piece of stone seven or eight inches tall and carved to look like a squid-bat-fish-man, it was heavier than it had any right to be and it kept getting heavier and heavier as we walked.

At last we reached the lake. The Washoes had boats there, flat-bottomed, square-prowed wooden things that would hardly draw any water. Nobody spoke, nor was there any need for anybody to speak. Abraham and I climbed into the boat and sat ourselves down. There were no seats in the boat, just the flat wooden floor or hull or whatever they call boat bottoms, and we sat there, Abraham facing front and me sitting behind him.

The Washoes climbed in behind us and pushed off from shore and started to paddle.

This was the strangest thing I had ever seen.

I looked over the edge of the boat and the water was so clear I couldn't see it at all. We seemed to be floating in air, propelled by the Washoes' paddles. The moonlight was so bright, the water so pure, I thought we were flying over the lake bottom.

And then I saw fish swimming beneath us. Gray Mackinaw and speckled rainbow trout, Kokanee salmon with their fancy red scales and cutthroats with their scales striped like tigers and spotted like leopards, and other things, great turtles, and less wholesome things, things with tentacles and claws and feelers like the ones that the little statue had on its face.

I felt something strike my face and thought it was burning me like acid until I realized that it was only water. It was water, splashed by one of the Washoes' paddles, so cold that my face didn't know whether it was scalding or freezing.

Nocturnal birds flew overhead casting their shadows on the lake that seemed to crawl along the bed, and then a great bird that shut us from the light of the moon and put us in total darkness for a moment until it passed off into the night. I watched it, a black, soaring shape that disappeared into the snow- and forest-covered mountains.

At last Abraham spoke, a single word in the Washoe language. I cannot repeat it, it was so strange my tongue won't get around it, but the Washoes dug their paddles into the clear water and our flat-bottomed boat glided to a halt.

And now the strangeness of the night became more strange and more strange yet.

Abraham stood up in the boat and signaled me to do likewise. I got carefully to my feet, not wishing to tip the boat and throw us all into the cold lake.

Before I could stop him, Abraham put one foot over the side of the boat and balanced carefully, one foot on the water and the other in the boat. And then he lifted his other foot, carefully but without hesitating, and he put it over the side as well, and stood beside the boat. Yes, he stood on the water.

He smiled at me and he held out one hand and I knew what he wanted me to do. I stood up and held the box in one hand and reached for him with the other, and when he took my hand I stepped over the side of the boat and stood beside Abraham ben Zaccheus the Hebrew King.

The Washoes paddled past us and I watched them swing their little flat-bottomed boat in a circle and head back for the shore.

The moon above looked as bright as the sun. The lake beneath our feet was clear and we could see the fishes and the other creatures going about their business, although one of the things with tentacles seemed to be awaiting a special treat.

The box with the statue in it seemed so heavy, I was not sure how much longer I could hold it. If I put it down would it float? Would it be carried away? Would it come to the shore and be hidden there, like little Moses in the bulrushes where Pharaoh's daughter found him so very long ago?

It grew suddenly dark again, and I looked up and saw that black shape pass across the face of the moon once again. I was not so sure, this time, that it was a bird.

Abraham reached with his free hand and jerked the bandanna from the stone statue in the box. I saw him tuck the bandanna back into his pocket. He released my hand with his, and I stood there on the water, wondering if this was the work of the Holy Spirit.

I looked down at the water and thought that it was invisible, and that the Holy Spirit was invisible, as well. The Holy Ghost. The greatest mystery, I had always believed, in the great mystery of the Holy Trinity.

That was another question that had got me a good clout from Father Phinean. Our priest was teaching us that God could do anything at all. There were no limits to His power. It was called *arm-nippy-tents*.

74

No limits? No limits at all?

No limits. That's what arm-nippy-tents means, you nasty boy, John O'Leary.

Could he make me invisible, Father?

Now what did I tell you, John? God can do anything. Of course he could make you invisible.

But then he couldn't see me, could he, Father?

He could if He wanted to.

But what if He wanted to make me so invisible even He couldn't see me, Father?

And why would He want to do such a ridiculous thing?

Well, Father, I don't know why, but what if He wanted to, could he make me so invisible He couldn't see me even if He wanted to see me?

Oh, Father Phinean looked flustered. He just about foamed at the mouth, he did. And then, ah, you know what happened then, don't you?

Of course you do.

The water must have been mightily cold; I marveled that it hadn't frozen over. There were flakes of snow whipping through the air, and back on the shore I could see some bits of orange where the Chinee village had burned and farther away the lights of the Tahoe Tavern, but here on the lake itself Abraham ben Zaccheus was standing as calm and steady as a bishop giving Holy Communion and I was standing there with him wondering what was keeping me from plunging straight down into that black, frigid body of water.

King Abraham pulled his thick winter gloves from his hands and shoved the gloves inside his coat. He reached for the stone statue in the box and grasped it with both hands and lifted it above his head.

The giant bird took another pass across the face of the moon and for just a moment we were in darkness there on the face of the lake, the only light the distant tavern and the Chinee village and the shining stars of the galaxy overhead. Then the statue flared with a light all its own. It sizzled there in Abraham's hands, held above Abraham's head, and then as if it had a life of its own it pulled itself forward and tipped head-downward and dived straight down into the water, pulling Abraham and me behind it.

As we hit the face of the lake it began to swirl and churn like the water in a wash-tub when the washer-woman pulls the plug. That glowing statue, I would tell you the color it glowed but it was something I had never in my life seen before and I can't to this day put a name to it, that statue pulled us along behind it, swirling and swooping in a cold whirl-pool, round and round, the only light the statue's glow. I looked over my shoulder and saw a tunnel through the water above us and the black sky and dancing stars at its end. I looked down and saw the waters opening before us like the Red Sea opening for the Children of Israel and I let go a prayer that we wouldn't wind up like Pharaoh's army.

There was a roaring in my ears and a great pinwheel of stars ahead of me and then with a thump we landed, Abraham and yours truly, standing there on a rocky plain surrounded by that whirling, roaring, funnel of water. A great fish whipped past and then one of those horrid things with the feelers and claws, distant relatives, I think of the ugly thing that I'd carried from the Chinee village in a wooden box.

The statue had landed with us and stood tilted a bit from the upright on its base. In front of us was something like nothing my eyes had ever before beheld. I could call it a city but it was like no city I'd ever seen, not Dublin nor London, England, nor Boston nor Chicago nor San Francisco. No, not even like the cities I'd seen only in pictures, not even the pillars and hanging gardens of Babylon or the pyramids and the Sphinx of Aegupt.

It hurt my eyes just to look at the city, and my stomach churned when I tried to understand its angles and its shapes. It wasn't the way a city should be. I couldn't tell what was wrong with it. The closest I can come is to say it was crooked, but it wasn't exactly that either. It was just wrong.

But it was little. It was like a tiny town set up in the window of Gump's Department Store on Post Street in San Francisco. The children would come to see that for a Christmas treat, and their parents would see the joy in their faces and it brought tears to my eyes when I thought that if Maeve Corrigan hadn't been kicked in the head by a cursed Englishman's horse we might have married when she was grown and had kiddies of our own that we could show a miniature city at Christmastime. There would be tiny houses and little trees and shops and mayhap even a miniature St. Padraic's. There would be tiny horses and sleighs, and a pond made of a mirror surrounded by white cotton snow.

Abraham was tugging at my sleeve. The village was growing before our eyes or we were shrinking, I could not tell. The thing on the statue was as tall as a man now or taller, or mayhap it was that Abraham and I had shriveled down to six inches or so of height so we were not even as tall as it.

The thing climbed down off its pedestal and began flopping and hopping across the black stone like a creature part frog and part fish, part squid and part man. The feelers that were its face were writhing and whipping like living things, and it was making a sound with what had to pass for its mouth that was fit neither for man nor beast nor anything else made by the loving God but only for something that crawled out of the pit of Gehenna to work a mission of damnation on the world.

The thing flopped through thoroughfares between horrid crooked blocks of spongy material that sagged and dripped like to make me puke back the fine meal I'd last consumed at the Tahoe Tavern. There was a stench in the air, and each step Abraham took or did I sent up a wet, squelching sound. Our footing had been solid black rock but now it, too, was spongy and unpleasant, as if the ground itself had become a greedy, living thing that with each step wanted to take hold on your foot and draw you down to a wet, dark, slimy Hell.

There was not a soul to be seen in the street, if this could be called a street, but there were sounds in the city that I would never wish to hear again if I live as long as Methuselah. There was a distant, watery chanting and the horrid, flopping thing moved faster, as if it couldn't wait to get to its destination.

At length we came to a great building that must have been a temple. It had columns outside and pilasters and a tall, frightening roof. I felt cold at its very sight and wanted to halt, but Abraham tugged me along and I was barely able to lift my boots from the hungry, sucking stuff we were walking upon.

The temple itself was filled with a congregation of thousands. I could scarcely believe my eyes. They were humans of a sort, some of them, but not proper humans. They were misshapen things, some with blank spaces where eyes should have been, some with broad, thin-lipped mouths that showed rows of glittering, triangular teeth when they opened them to hiss. There were some with scaly skins, or skins of a color no proper human had ever sported, or with horrid, flattened heads that would leave little room for a brain, or with eyes in the palms of their hands that they held up and pointed at us as we followed the thing that had been a statue toward the front of their temple.

The thing pulled itself up onto a dais and turned to face the room. The throng assembled sent up a chant, horrid, discordant words in language that deserved to be blasted from all human recollection, and then the beast before them seemed to swell, its belly like the obscene womb of a monstrous Madonna preparing to give birth to, I swear it, naught less than the anti-Christ itself.

As the thousands chanted, the monstrosity reared back on its clawed legs and spread its scaly wings with a terrible *snap!* That sent a fetid wind that was a stench in my nostrils and that stung my eyes like acid. It began to sing and the sound of its voice, unbearably lovely, yes, lovely, was more than I could tolerate.

I launched myself at it then, prepared to tear that horrid thing to bits with my bare hands, to rip out its throat with my very teeth as some ancestor of mine prowling the woods of ancient Ireland might have torn out the throats of some half-human monstrosity.

And then, suddenly, all was well. I

might have seen the thing reach out to me with its slimy feelers but in the instant that it touched my flesh I was all right. It was as if I were a babe once more, and the thing holding me was nestling me like a loving mother. It touched my face. I looked up at it and it looked down at me, and I saw love in its eyes, and peace. I saw that tiny village with its little wooden horses pulling little painted wagons, its mirror lake and cotton snow, and children playing.

There were children playing. They were running and sliding on the ice, throwing snow at one another, and someone had built a snowman beside the lake and stuck a carrot for its nose and an old hat atop its head. A few flakes were falling and we were shouting and joking, Rogan and Seamus and Malachy, Shane Galloway and Glenna Lynch and Maeve, and I ran across the ice to Maeve and took her in my arms and kissed her and she laughed and pushed me away and scolded me for behaving like a masher and a voice was sounding far away only to come closer.

A voice.

It was reciting, and it had a religious tone to it. I wondered if it was Father Phinean come to warn us all that the day was growing late and it was time to head to our homes so our fathers and mothers wouldn't worry too much about us.

But it wasn't Father Phinean's voice, it was another voice, and each word struck me like a hammer blow.

Aa!

Aah!

Aalu!

Ab!

Abaddon!

Abaris!

I knew now what the voice was speaking.

Abdiel!

Abelios!

Abellio!

Abeona!

I knew, and each word was like the blow of a hammer upon my skull. It was a pain inside my mind and inside my soul, a searing fiery pain and yet I knew that someone was struggling to save me.

I heard the chanting that had welcomed our little procession into the temple, and the song of the monster, its voice as dear as a mother's, its song as sweet as a lullaby and I was drawn to it once more, drawn into peace and contentment and darkness.

But the other voice persisted.

Abog!

Abracadabra!

Abraxas!

Abundantia!

Someone was reciting the names of the gods.

Acheloüs!

Acheron!

Achilles!

Achor!

They were gods of good and gods of evil, gods of the Greeks and of the Romans, the Cretans and the Persians. They were pulling me away from the darkness and the foul joy that the monster offered me. I felt the monster's squid-like tentacles draw my face into it, and I was lifted up the tunnel of water and into the black sky a million miles from Earth.

I saw stars and comets. I saw creatures that could travel between the worlds and between the suns. Creatures that looked like insects or like worms, like great whales that swam in the very emptiness of space, like flying cones with star-shaped heads and a million tentacles trailing behind them for millions of miles. I could be one of them, something whispered to me, I could live with them forever. I could give them the Earth and they could come there and feast on Men, not on their flesh but on their minds.

Kalki!
Kalma!
Kama!
Kami!
Kamui!
Kari!
Karttikeya!

Gods of Japan. Gods of India. Gods of Africa. Gods of the island people.

Xilonen!
Xipetotec!
Xochiquetzal!
Yahweh!

The monster-mother-mother-monster-monster-mother shuddered.

Yahweh! the voice repeated. Yahweh! Yahweh!

There was a horrid bubbling and burbling. My face and then my entire body felt as if I were being bathed in boiling, burning mud. I opened my eyes and saw the face of the monster as it flung me from it, flung me at Abraham ben Zaccheus.

Around us the temple was shrinking, the worshippers fleeing for their lives. The monster that had held me in its claws was shriveling, shriveling, diminishing until it was only seven or eight inches tall, and slumped back onto a little square pedestal where it crouched, its wings folded behind its back, its elbows resting wearily on its knees.

There are kings everywhere, God the King of Universe and for all my money this thing, this monstrous lovely terrible little statue was the King of Hell.

The sucking, spongy stuff beneath our feet began to churn and suck the dreadful things down into the blackness and the muck that lay below the lake, but Abraham ben Zaccheus and John O'Leary did not go below with those things.

With a rending sound Abraham and I burst through the roof of the temple. The city lay in ruins around our booted feet, a city no larger than the Christmas scene on display on Post Street for the pleasure of the city's children.

Propelled by some invisible force, Abraham ben Zaccheus and I rushed upward through the swirling whirlpool. Luminous fish stared at us with their great eyes, turtles swam by, the shape of their mouths making them seem to laugh at our plight.

We flew into the air, then fell back, shattering the smooth surface of the lake. Behind us, the whirlpool slowed and filled in and disappeared. Above us the night had passed, the breeze brought a few stray snowflakes into our faces. The sun was high overhead, and bright and clean.

A flat-bottomed boat stood nearby. Washoe Indians paddled it toward us, helped us carefully over the gunwales so as not to swamp the little boat, then headed back toward shore.

The Tahoe Tavern was bustling with fine visitors from Reno to the East, Sacramento and even distant San Francisco to the West. I hoped the management had saved our room. I hoped that my new friend was still staying at the Tavern. I wondered whether I ought tell her my story, and whether she would believe it if I did.

Steps Leading Downward

They play a splendid game here in America. Base Ball is its name, and if I have the sense to say that the sun will rise tomorrow, you can believe me when I tell you that this is the grandest game ever devised out of human ingenuity. They play it whenever the weather permits, and it being March in this Year of Our Lord One Thousand Nine Hundred and Six, and what with the lovely mild climate of this city and the fact that spring is well upon us, the lads are swarming the diamonds and the sound of wooden shillelaghs whacking leathern spheres is heard at every hand.

I tell you, those spoiled and spavined English with their game named for a harmless insect have lost another one, and well do they deserve it. If you ask me. Or my name is not John Fergus Tiernan O'Leary. And that is indeed my true name, you can take it from me.

90

Mr. Abraham ben Zaccheus, my generous employer and secretly the King of the Hebrews as well as Apostolic Emperor of Austria and Hungary and a few dozen other fancy titles, did not need me this day, so I took myself to a vacant lot where a group of lads were playing this Base Ball and watched them go at it for a while. At first the game is a bit hard to follow, but the fact of the matter is that I am an unusually bright young fellow, and with the aid of a gaggle of kids who were watching the proceedings and cheering on one team or the other, I soon caught on to how it works.

All to the good, as in the midst of everything a most attractive young lady arrives upon the scene. She stands watching, too, for a little while. Then the players score something called the 'third out' and go rushing to exchange places, the fellows who had been standing about waiting to catch the ball instead setting themselves on a wooden bench while another group who had been sitting on another bench leap to their feet and run to take their places on the field.

All except for the fellow who runs to pick up the shillelagh that another player had dropped after making the 'third out.' This new player waves the shillelagh in the air and yells at the fellow standing in the middle of the field to go ahead and throw the ball at him. Another fellow is squatting on the ground in a most distressing pose, waiting for the fellow in the middle of the field to throw the ball. Should he miss the player with the shillelagh in his hand, as I've seen happen before, the other lad will catch it if he can and throw it back to the first fellow for another try.

The player with the shillelagh in his hand, in the meanwhile, can use the shillelagh to defend himself against the ball if it comes too close to him.

Well, now, as I told you, this young lady having arrived and observed the proceedings for a bit, walks over to the fellow squatting on the ground and grabs him by one ear. She gives it a twist that would have made a banshee howl and drags the poor lad to his feet.

She begins berating him something awful, I dare not even try to repeat some of the words she uses, but the drift of her tirade is this: He was due home an hour ago at least. She expected to find him in a saloon and has visited a dozen or so of such establishments, finding there most of his friends but no sign of her victim himself.

Aha!, she says to herself, I know where that rapscallion must have got himself to. He's playing a game of Base Ball with a bunch of other wastrels, and indeed here you are and you're coming home with me this minute and do your duties around the house.

Those duties she does not specify, nor will I dare to speculate upon them. Use your own imagination and do not rely on me to do your work for you.

The job of 'catcher' on a Base Ball team, I quickly learned, was simple. The 'pitcher' throws the ball and if he misses the 'batter' or the batter defends himself with his shillelagh or 'bat,' then the other players have to deal with the matter. If the pitcher misses both batter and bat, the catcher retrieves the ball and returns it to the pitcher.

A wee lad could understand that!

But after a while the other team gets three men on the 'bases' and the batter wallops the ball between a couple of 'outfielders,' and next thing I know these fellows are racing around the footpath as if Satan himself was after them with a blowtorch aimed at their fundaments. They come whizzing right past me. An outfielder throws the ball to an 'infielder' who throws it to me and when the next fellow comes running I'm supposed to put a touch on him with the ball.

Are you following me?

We never had anything like this in Kilkee, I can tell you.

Well I'm standing there with the ball in my hand and a big bruiser in canvas trousers and mighty brogans is charging down upon me. All of a sudden, instead of running on, he leaps in the air, feet first, and we collide with a mighty whack.

Then we fall to the ground and he's mad as a wet hen and I'm not in the friendliest of moods myself, having been kicked in the middens with this fellow's size twelves. We go rolling around exchanging greetings in the form of knuckles and knees, and the 'umpire' starts yelling at us.

Oh, I didn't tell you about the umpire. He's a kind of presiding judge in the game of Base Ball.

Anyway, the umpire starts yelling at the both of us and waving his arms, and pretty soon he's got his face uncomfortably close to mine so I give him a nice taste of my fist and before I know it everybody is piling on and there's the most glorious free-for-all you can imagine.

The fellows on my team must have appreciated everything I did for them, because they gave me one of those shillelaghs that they use to whack the ball as a gift, and I took it away with me and brought it back to King Abraham's house with me. Oh, if I get another chance I'm going back and join one of those Base Ball 'clubs' as they call them. It is a wondrous grand sport, is this Base Ball.

But I get back to King Abraham's

house on Rooshian Hill and I'll admit I was looking a wee bit battered and bedraggled so I went and washed up and put on some clean clothing. I came back to the parlor where Abraham was, as usual, studying one of the musty books from his grand personal library. The sun had set and he had the gaslights going.

He looked up as I entered and closed the heavy book he'd been reading.

'John O'Leary, have you dined?'

'I have not,' I admitted. 'Will the splendid Xiang Xu-Mei be preparing a repast tonight?'

Abraham smiled at my pronunciation of his housekeeper's name. Mayhap my tongue had a bit of trouble with the Chinee words. I did not take issue, however, with my employer. He makes a gesture with one hand toward the telephone machine that he keeps in his parlor.

'I had a call from a gentleman in need of help,' he said. 'We are invited to dine with him at the Palace.'

Ahah! I said to myself, King Abraham has slipped up at last. Clever scholar though he is, he always denies his royal status and lives in this modest house, but now he has given himself away. Thinking that at last I will get to see his royal court, I told him that I was delighted to be included in the invitation.

'Run a comb through your hair and put on your best jacket, then.' He pulled his brass turnip from his weskit pocket, studied its face, and announced, 'We have barely time to meet him.'

Very well, then. A few minutes passed and I found myself seated besides Abraham in his electric buggy, gliding silently down Rooshian Hill toward Market Street. We pulled into the carriage court of the Palace, all right, and a mighty vizier costumed like the tenor in a grand opera greeted us. A lackey drove Abraham's electric buggy away while the mighty vizier escorted us into the Palace.

It was indeed the grandest building I had ever set foot in. The floors were marble and the ceilings were gold. There were tapestries on the walls and Persian carpets underfoot. There were lovely women in gorgeous gowns and elegant gentlemen in fine outfits that made me almost ashamed to be seen in my plain working man's get-up.

But I was in the company of his Apostolic Majesty, Abraham ben Zaccheus I, by the Grace of God, Emperor of Austria, King of Hungary and Bohemia and also King of the Hebrews, and if my outfit was all right with King Abraham then no man would dast say me no, I was certain of that.

We were escorted to our table, a glittering set-up surrounded by others equally as glittering. Stained glass overhead was no less splendid than you'd find in a cathedral. I glanced at the diners at the other tables, expecting them to rise and make obeisance to King Abraham, but they went on as if nothing out of the ordinary had happened.

A little orchestra was pumping away at the works of some dead Eye-Tallian fellow, and they continued their labors as we were seated. The conductor turned around and winked at King Abraham. He was a real sight, that orchestra conductor, looked like a Goliath up there with a big pompadour of hair and a moustache and a beard, shoulders out to here and a grin befitting the cat that drank the cream. He turned away and went back to his conducting. Winking at the king, what an amazing place this San Francisco is.

And for an Apostolic Emperor, King Abraham was a mighty democratic monarch!

There was a fellow already sitting at our table and he got up and shook hands with Abraham. Abraham told him my name and he told me his. It was Amos bar Kiva. We all sat down and a waiter came over and poured us some wine and we talked a little about the weather and President Rosey Velt and Governor Pardee and Mayor Schmitz, the head man of this splendid city, and what a grand job everybody was doing. But Mr. bar Kiva seemed like a man under a dark cloud. I wondered what was the matter.

After we'd downed a little of our wine Abraham turned toward me and said that Mr. bar Kiva was a member of the Ohabai Shalome Synagogue on Bush Street and that he was a Shepherd, which

I know what that is, except King Abraham said that a Shepherd was a special kind of Hebrew from Spain or Italy and Mr. bar Kiva was in fact from the city of Milan in Italy. In his honor we were going to have an Eye-Tallian feast for our dinner.

Upon the which our waiter brought out a little appetizer consisting of some grilled and marinated vegetables, cured salami, olives, roasted nuts, garbanzo beans, olive oil and rosemary soup, a pretty salad of bitter Eye-Tallian greens, some roasted pancetta, walnuts, and Balsamic vinegar.

I thought that was most tasty and it did indeed serve to buck up my appetite.

While the waiter traipsed off to bring us our meal, King Abraham talked Mr. bar Kiva into telling us what was making him such an unhappy fellow.

'Something is happening to our congregation,' he said. 'People are disappearing from the temple. Now they're becoming afraid, and attendance is falling off.'

He didn't say it exactly like that, understand. As an Eye-Tallian fellow he had a peculiar way of talking, not properly the way Father Phinean taught us to speak at St. Padraic's back in Kilkee, but it wasn't Mr. bar Kiva's fault that he was a Hebrew Shepherd and not a good Irishman like myself or a King like Mr. Abraham ben Zaccheus.

It was Mr. bar Kiva, it turned out, who had called Abraham on the telephone machine and talked him into coming to the Palace to meet him for dinner. Imagine, a king needing an invitation to take a meal at his own Palace!

Three members of the congregation of Ohabai Shalome had disappeared. All of them had disappeared while going down into the basement of the synagogue to bring up some food that the women of the congregation had prepared down there. The cooks were there already. The women went down to get the food. Several members of the synagogue had seen them go down downstairs, but the women in the kitchen said they never arrived.

The first woman to disappear was a recent bride, married less than a year. Her name was Joaquina Ha-Nagid. Her husband had lived in San Francisco all his life. He had written to relatives in Barcelona, sending money for a young virgin to travel to this city to be his wife.

'Did they get along well?' Abraham ben Zaccheus asked Amos bar Kiva.

'What do you mean?'

'I mean, was she happy? The young woman — she was young, was she not?'

'Little more than a child. She married at age fifteen. She had celebrated her sixteenth birthday just the week before her disappearance.'

'One so young, thousands of miles from her home and family. She might have run away.'

'I think not.'

Abraham ben Zaccheus raised his heavy, dark eyebrows. 'Why so?'

'She seemed happy with her husband. He is a gentle man, known for his kindness and charity. He is a dry goods merchant. He was twelve years her senior. Joaquina was expecting a child.'

'Ah, ah, yes.' Abraham nodded. He reached for a loaf of dark bread, tore off a piece and dipped it in olive oil. He chewed on it meditatively, then said, 'The prospective parents, they were pleased?'

'Delighted. Her husband, Yeshurun, had married once before and his wife died in a fire. He hardly moved for seven years, except to go to work and to go to *Shul*. When he finally decided to marry again he sent for a bride and Joaquina came. All he could talk about in recent months was the coming baby.'

'And the wife, Joaquina, she was happy, also?'

'Thrilled. She spent all her time sewing clothes for the infant. She wanted to name it for her grandfather or her grandmother, both dead and buried in Spain.'

Abraham ben Zaccheus rubbed his face with his hand. 'What food were they preparing that night, Amos?'

'You expect me to remember that? This was an occasion of tragedy. A young woman, a bride, a mother-to-be disappears, and you ask me what was for dinner that night?'

'Please,' Abraham said, 'try to remember.'

A cloud passed over Amos bar Kiva's face. His eyes peered into the past, seeing that past occasion. His nostrils twitched and I imagined him smelling the food.

'There was *sopa de avikas*, Abraham, made with beef, olive oil, onions, garlic, tomatoes, pepper and lemon wedges. There was a roasted eggplant salad. And the main dish, Abraham, was *sogliole ai limone* . . . '

Abraham turned toward me and said, 'Sole with lemon, John.'

'With sea salt,' Amos said, 'wine and fish stock, olive oil and lemon juice and chopped parsley.'

'Good, good.' Abraham was tapping on the fine linen tablecloth with his fingers. 'Good. And the other time? When the other pregnant women disappeared, Amos — what food was being prepared in the synagogue?'

'Abraham, does it matter?'

'It matters very much!' Abraham ben Zaccheus is a soft-spoken man most of the time, but he had changed suddenly.

'Yes,' Amos said. 'All right. Let me remember. Yes, all right. On the other occasion it was *papeyada di berenjena*. You know this dish, Abraham? It was brought by a member of our congregation from the town of Edirne, Turkey. Fried eggplant with sugar. Delicious. A wonderful appetizer.'

'And then?'

'Then, let me recall. Yes. *Peshkado Avramila*, poached fish with Abraham's fruit. The women used whole salmon for this, with large tart fresh plums and red wine.'

'Yes.' Abraham stopped him with a gesture. 'Fish. Always fish.'

'I don't see why that matters.'

'Of course not. The fish gods, Amos. So many peoples have fish gods. The Babylonian Dagon, the Greek Poseidon, the Roman Neptune. Think of the tales of mermaid and mermen, of harpies and sea-witches. The goddess Yemoja of the Umbandists, the god Olokun, Nommo, Enki, the Chinese Fu Hsi, the Hindu Vishnu, the Philistines' Atargis, Nereus, Oe of Babylon, Iris and Electra. And that's just the beginning. There is evil, Amos. Evil beneath the sea and evil beneath the earth. Who knows what was summoned, what beings followed the creatures of the sea to Ohabai Shalome.'

Now it was Amos who looked troubled.

Abraham asked, 'Was there a smell of the sea left behind when the women were stolen? Was there a trail of water?'

Amos bar Kiva was nearly in tears. He put a hand to his brow. He whispered, 'There was. There was a trace of water on the stairs. There was an odor. I thought it was from the cooking, but it might have been more of a fresh sea odor.'

Ben Zaccheus muttered something I could not make out.

The orchestra was playing a tune now, something I recognized. I'd heard this one in a Barbary Coast melodeon and I was surprised to hear it played by a fine orchestra here in the Palace. Of course there was nobody singing but I knew the tune just the same. It was *A Woman Is Only a Woman but a Good Cigar is a Smoke*. Ah, it made me smile to hear it but I thought that big orchestra leader with his fancy pompadour must have a mighty nerve on him.

106

Between bites of truly excellent food and sips of a variety of wines, my employer was continuing to question Mr. bar Kiva. It was a good thing that I had read some of Dr. Doyle's fine stories. I suspected that Abraham ben Zaccheus had, as well, for I could almost hear the great detective's voice as he spoke.

'What time was it, that Mrs. Ha-Nagid disappeared?'

'Why — I'm not certain. It was a social evening at the synagogue, Mr. ben Zaccheus. It wasn't Shabbat or any special day of the calendar.'

'Save that every day the Divine One gives us is special,' Abraham commented.

'I think the men were upstairs in the great hall, the women were preparing food, Joaquina was carrying dishes up from the kitchen. She had just set some out and went back for more. When she didn't return, her husband worried. He went downstairs, he said he was afraid she was feeling ill, but the other women had never seen her.'

Abraham put his hand to his beard, the thumb on one side and fingers on the other, and drew downward, a thoughtful expression on his face.

'It was after dark, then, eh?'

'Yes.'

'The synagogue has gaslights.'

'We plan to install electricity but had not done so as yet.'

'They were lit?'

'Yes. Otherwise the sanctuary would be very dim after sunset, and the basement would be pitch black.'

'I've been in Ohabai Shalome many times, of course, but I'll want to retrace Joaquina Ha-Nagid's steps.'

'Of course.'

At this point the waiter brought our next course, a most delicious Tuscan roasted rack of lamb, served with Bucatini pasta, garlic, red onions, stewed tomatoes, zucchini, hot chilies, mint jelly and freshly baked Tuscan rolls, roasted garlic and olive oil.

Informal though it was, the Palace served a most admirable dinner. It was fit for a king, and it was my pleasure to be King Abraham's guest.

King Abraham lifted a Tuscan roll,

broke it in half and dipped one piece in olive oil. He chewed it thoughtfully. Then he sipped some wine. The orchestra had changed its tune. I recognized its new ditty as another I'd heard in a melodeon along the Barbary Coast. It was *Rufus Rastus Johnson Brown*, a funny tune indeed.

'Now, then' Abraham said, 'you tell me there were three disappearances.'

'Correct.'

'Who were the other two victims?'

'They were two cousins. Two more married women, although not as young as Mrs. Ha-Nagid. There was Liviya Navon ibn Gabirol, wife of Shamir the furniture maker, and there was Nitza Shazar-Suleiman, wife of Tsadek the tailor. In fact the women were cousins, daughters of two sisters. They were both between twenty and twenty-five years of age.'

'They disappeared the same night as Joaquina?'

'No. It was some weeks later. Again, they disappeared from the staircase leading from the sanctuary to the basement, to the kitchen.'

'Also at night?'

'Yes.'

Abraham cut a generous slice of lamb, speared it with his fork, dipped it in mint jelly and conveyed it to his mouth. I watched him chew, his eyes fixed on some invisible chimera. He seemed oblivious to the music of the orchestra and the hundreds of diners surrounding our table.

A party of San Francisco matrons observed us from a nearby table. I thought they must be watching the king, but one of them caught my eye instead. She wore her reddish hair in a stylish upsweep, and a high-collared gown that did little to conceal her most attractive figure. Kilkee would have been scandalized by such a wench, and by the daring look she shot my way, but in this city one was free to act as one wished. I returned her look and we exchanged nods.

The orchestra had commenced to play a tune called *Razzazza Mazzazza* and I couldn't help myself but to visit the party of ladies and ask one of them to join me for a dance. To my delight she consented, and I led her out to join the other dancers. At the end of a most delightful whirl across the polished floor I escorted her to her table once more. As we parted she managed to slip something into my hand. It turned out to be her calling card, complete with address and telephone number. I slipped it into my breast pocket as I rejoined Abraham ben Zaccheus and Amos bar Kiva at our own table. I was mightily pleased.

My employer and his companion had continued to discuss the mystery of the disappearing women. By now they were up to the dates of the disappearances. Although they spoke in English, there were words of Hebrew now and then that were puzzling to my ear.

'The first disappearance, that of Mrs. Ha-Nagid, took place on *yon shlishi*, the third day after the first *Shabbos* of *Shvat*. The other tragedies, the disappearances of Mrs. ibn Gabirol and Mrs. Shaza-Suleiman, took place on the eve of the third *Shabbos* of *Shvat*.'

'And the circumstances were just the same?' Abraham asked.

Before Amos bar Kiva answered, the

waiter appeared to clear our table and bring the next course, a fine dish of swordfish studded with garlic and smothered in a sauce of green olives and oranges. There were more roasted vegetables and rice, and a fresh bottle of local wine.

Amos bar Kiva nodded.

'Yes. The women were preparing food in the basement of the synagogue, in the kitchen there. On the first occasion, Mrs. Ha-Nagid left the sanctuary to go to the kitchen. The women there say that she never arrived, nor had she been seen since. On the second occasion, Mrs. ibn Gabirol and Mrs. Shazar-Suleiman left the sanctuary to bring food from the kitchen.'

He paused to lift his wine glass to his lips, then resumed.

'The first incident had of course been the chief topic of conversation ever since Joaquina had disappeared. Tongues wagged, I must admit. But Liviya and Nitza told some of the men that they would go together to the kitchen, so that whatever demon had seized Joaquina would be confused by the presence of two women at once, and they could escape his grasp.'

Abraham ben Zaccheus grunted. He held out a hand, interrupting Amos bar Kiva.

'And what demon would that be?'

Amos bar Kiva shrugged, a bemused expression on his face. 'I don't believe in demons, Abraham.'

'Nor do I,' Abraham replied, and then, after a pause, 'except when I do. They have a smell, Amos, did you know that? Demons have a smell all their own, and I have detected it in this city in recent times. I detect it coming from beneath the ground, and if the women disappeared underground I would not laugh at the theory that a demon was responsible.'

'Nonsense.'

'Not nonsense, my friend. There are demons who will deceive men and the children of men. There are demons who try to fool us. They masquerade as gods. That is why the Sublime One has commanded us to have no other god before Him. He has seen what those demons do, and He gives us warning.'

Again, Amos indicated his disbelief.

Abraham said, 'Listen to me, Amos bar Kiva. Even a simple soul like my dear helper John O'Leary knows enough to beware of demons. Don't you, John?'

'Of a certainty,' I replied. I was enjoying the broiled lamb and mint jelly myself, accompanied by small roasted potatoes and morsels of the fine freshly baked sourdough bread, all of it washed down with a very pleasant wine. But I did indeed know that demons were dangerous. That was one of the few lessons of Father Phinean at home in Kilkee that I ever found sensible.

'Every race has its God or its many gods,' Abraham asserted. He reached across the table and poked at Amos bar Kiva's shirt to emphasize his point. 'You'll notice that even the Almighty One, the King of the Universe, does not tell us that there are no other gods, only that we must have no other god before Him.'

Amos, I must say, was looking ashen. As for me, I thought Abraham made good sense, but then I've always been ready to listen to people who sound as if they know what they're talking about, whether they do or not. And Abraham, well, you don't get to be King of the Jews, not to mention Apostolic Emperor of Austria and Hungary and all those other things that Abraham was, without learning a lesson or two. I'm not saying that I believed him, understand, but I was assuredly willing to listen.

'Kumarbis,' he was saying, 'Kumarbis was important to the Hittites and the Hurrites, Amos. We don't hear much of him any more, nor of the Hittites and the Hurrites for that matter, do we? Do you know the *Song of Ullikummis*? Do you know the *Royalty in the Skies*? We have our holy *Pentateuch*, Amos. John O'Leary has his *Four Gospels*. The Hittites and the Hurrites had the *Cycle of Kumarbis*.'

'You know too much, Abraham.' Amos bar Kiva had put down his knife and fork. He held onto the edge of the fine linen tablecloth with his knobby hands. 'You know so much that it confuses you.'

Abraham shook his head. 'Listen to

me,' he told Amos, 'listen to this. I have read as much as is known of the *Cycle of Kumarbis*. Let me see if I can summon up a few snatches from my cobwebby memory.'

He closed his eyes and threw back his head, then opened his eyes again so suddenly there was almost an audible *snap*. It was an odd gesture I had seen him make on occasion. It was as if he was looking for some kind of message, something written in invisible letters across the sky. Then he spoke in a voice so different from his usual, I wondered if it was really Abraham speaking or one of those clever ventrilly quists which perform betimes at the melodeons.

Come, Impaluris! Kumarbis, father of the gods, summons you to the house of the gods. The Issirra will take the child and will convey him to the dark Earth.

Then Impaluris took his staff and set forth. He betook himself to the Issirra. He spoke the same words to them that had been spoken to him by Kumarbis. But you are not to know his motive in summoning you. Hasten, come!

When the Issirra heard these words they hastened, they hurried. They set forth and covered ground without stopping once. They presented themselves to Kumarbis and Kumarbis spoke to them. 'Take this child and take it away with you. Bring it down to the dark Earth! Be quick! Place it like an arrow on the right shoulder of Upelluris. In one day it shall increase a cubit. In one month it shall increase an acre.'

When the Issirra heard these words they took the child from Kumarbis's lap. They took him and placed him in Enlil's lap. The god raised his eyes and saw the child as it stood in his divine presence.

Enlil said to himself in his soul, 'Who is this? Are they really the goddesses of fate who have raised him? Is it he who shall see the fierce battles of the great gods? By none other than Kumarbis is this vileness done. Just as he raised the storm god, so he has now raised this terrible man of pryoxene as his rival!'

Abraham stopped. The orchestra was playing a merry tune. The ladies at the table nearby were staring.

So was Amos bar Kiva.

'What are you saying, Abraham? What do you mean?'

Abraham had a dazed look on his face, like Malachy Teague back in Kilkee when he insulted my darling Maeve Corrigan, she of pleasant memory, and I cold-cocked him and he wound up sitting on the turf with blood running from his nose and me standing above him asking if he wanted some more of the same, which offer, being a sensible fellow and one of my dearest friends, he declined with thanks.

But I was telling you about Abraham ben Zaccheus, His Majesty, and the dinner conversation he was having with his Hebrew friend Amos bar Kiva. And after a sip of cold water Abraham's face regained its normal expression and he resumed his enlightening of Amos, to which I listened as well, as you can see that I must have, lest I not be able to go on with my tale.

'I have studied the religions of the world,' Abraham resumed. 'They are marvelous in their color and infinite in their variety, Amos. But at the same time they so often have similarities to one another, one is inclined to think they are all memories of the same truth. Faded and distorted by the passage of centuries, to be sure. But at their heart, true.'

'The Divine One forbids us,' Amos broke in.

'Indeed He does, Amos. I'm sure He will forgive my frail efforts to rescue his children who have been stolen away by His enemies.'

Amos bar Kiva looked grim but he said, 'Very well, Abraham. Go on. Who are these Impaluris and Upalluris and Kumarbis and Enlil and Issirra?'

Abraham waited while a fellow in a white jacket cleared off our table and carted off the debris of our meal. A waiter brought a pot of coffee and couple of bottles of the management's best whiskey and a platter of little cakes and another of apples and oranges and grapes. Oh, they eat very well in this city of San Francisco, I can tell you that.

'The Hurrites in particular had an interesting pantheon,' Abraham said. I make it a point to remember the words he uses that I've never heard before, and *pantheon* was one of them. I always use Abraham's big Webster's Dictionary when I get back to Rooshian Hill and look them up. I am improving myself every day, here in America. They would be amazed in old Kilkee, were I ever to pay a visit to my little home.

'They worshipped in something called a *kuntarra*, not so different from our synagogue or a Muslim mosque. You need not worry about their different gods just now, Amos, although I find the study of all religions rewarding. The point is that the Issirra were their elder gods, who came before Kumarbis and the rest. The Greeks and the Romans had a similar notion, with Titans who gave way to their own gods.'

'You are not going to say that the Divine One was the child of an older race, Abraham!' Amos looked scandalized.

'On the contrary. Our Christian friends have their notions about Yehoshua ben Miryam wa Yosef, they call him Jesus the

Son of God. Is that not so, John O'Leary?'

'And also King of the Jews,' I said, 'according to Father Phinean.'

'Ah, Father Phinean. I've heard so much from you about that good man that I feel as if I know him, John O'Leary. I think we would have many a fine debate.'

'Well, I doubt greatly that Father Phinean will ever come to San Francisco, Abraham.'

'But I might find myself in Kilkee sometime, John. We never know about these things, do we?'

'Indeed we do not, Abraham.' I peeled myself a fine fat orange, as round and lovely to look upon as a dear part of a woman, and as delicious to taste as well. I popped a section of the fruit in my mouth and savored its juice, then followed it with a sip of fine Scotch whiskey, not as good as our fine Irish whisky, but still satisfactory, especially considering the price I was paying. The water of life and the juice of the fruit make a fine combination, I promise. Try them some time and if you don't agree with me then my name is not John O'Leary, late of Village Kilkee, of the Kingdom of Ireland, yet to be restored.

'Gods and children of gods, sometimes rivals of gods, sometimes in rebellion against the gods, Amos.'

Abraham was pointing his finger at the other fellow. A stubby finger it was, at that, as fits a stubby man such as Abraham ben Zaccheus. But there was a power in that finger as there was in that man. I would not want that finger pointed at me in scorn, nor would I want to come up against Abraham ben Zaccheus in any kind of struggle, for all that I stood over him by the better part of a foot and outweighed him by half again, and all of my pounds solid muscle.

'Most of the world's religions speak of realms beneath the Earth, as well, Amos, or of realms in the sky. The Egyptians sent Pharaoh, cursed be he, to the sun god and the sky goddess in a boat. The dead of the Greeks were carried to Hades on the boat of Charon. And the Hurrites — the Hurrites — what did they say? *'Take this child and take it away with you. Bring it down to the dark Earth! Be quick!'* Did they mean to bring a child of the gods to the world of Man, Amos? Or did they mean to take a child of Man to the world below? I think the gods of the Hurrites are stirring, Amos. I think the gods of the Hurrites, Kumarbis, Impalluris and the rest, are still at war with the Issirra. And those foul gods, those demons, are stealing babies from the very wombs of the daughters of the Sublime One, blessed be His name.'

The orchestra had stopped playing lively tunes and gone back to that drab frog music or kraut music, as if any sensible man could tell the difference or would even want to. The big, good-looking leader had left the bandstand and some little dried-up longhaired fellow had taken his place. The big fellow was making his way across the room, stopping to shake hands and slap backs like a politician.

He arrived at our table and shook hands with Abraham and Amos. Abraham introduced me to him, and the big fellow identified himself as Eugene Schmitz, proud leader of the Union Labor Party and Lord Mayor of the City of San Francisco. I stood up and clasped his mitt in my own and he gave a mighty squeeze and I gave a mightier one and we stood there for a bit seeing who could squeeze the other's mitt the harder.

I think the fellow thought he could get the best of me so to teach him a thing or two I reached down with my free hand and picked up a section of juicy orange and popped it in my mouth, grinning away at Eugene there who was turning red and starting to sweat. Well, thought I, it would be unkind to embarrass His Highness the Lord Mayor so I let go his hand and told him I was proud to make his acquaintanceship and would give him all my votes the next time he needed them.

He thanked me politely, then drew up a chair without even being invited and joined our little party. It turned out that His Honor the Lord Mayor was an acquaintance of King Abraham, not a surprising turn of events, and that he also knew Mr. Amos bar Kiva. I felt like the odd man out at this point, so I excused myself and made my way to a nearby table. I asked one of the ladies sitting there if she would care to trip the light fantastic with me, and she agreed to do so.

If the orchestra had been playing some merry tune like *Jim Judson from the Town of Hackensack* or even a sentimental ditty like *Where the River Shannon Flows* I would have been pleased, but they were scratching away at some Eye Tally Anne tune. Even so, the lady and I managed to enjoy ourselves sufficiently that she suggested a repeat, and then invited me to join her and her friends.

Well, not wishing to be impolite to the King and the Lord Mayor, I asked leave to speak briefly with them. The Lord Mayor and Mr. bar Kiva allowed as how they were delighted to have made my acquaintance. King Abraham said that he would need my services on the morrow but suggested that I have myself a good time tonight, and so I made a polite bow (so as not to have to wreck the Lord Mayor's mitt with another handshake) and did indeed join my new lady friend and her party.

My new friend's name was Taryn Jilleen O'Casey. I knew right off, of course, that she had to be a daughter of the sod, for all that she was born right here in San Francisco. She had the midnight hair and lovely dark complexion of the Black Irish, aye, descended, as our tales have it, from the shipwrecked sailors of the mighty Spanish Armada who washed upon the shores of our island and joined their race to ours. Hair as black and shiny as a raven's wing, skin like a baby's and eyes the color of a stormy sea.

Ah, such a girl was this Taryn Jilleen O'Casey!

She might dine and dance with the swells but she was a self-supporting working girl, a typewriter in a lawyer's office. She lived in a lovely flat on Tellygraph Hill, not so far from Abraham ben Zaccheus's digs on Rooshian Hill, and I will say nothing more about the next few hours for I am a man of utter discretion, not given in the least to kissing and telling, any more than I am to fighting or to boasting, as you of course already know.

When I returned to King Abraham's digs on Rooshian Hill, His Majesty's housekeeper, Xiang Xu-Mei, prepared me a delightful repast which I consumed in the parlor, watching the world go by the windows of King Abraham's house. This was a dandy way to earn my living, indeed. I was a trifle weary. Taryn Jilleen O'Casey has worn me out before serving me a splendid breakfast of bacon and eggs, muffins and grapefruit and spicy tea.

Two meals into the day I heard the voice of my employer summoning me to his library. The walls there were covered with books, more I imagine than there were in the entire village of Kilkee. Abraham ben Zaccheus had taken down some of the biggest books, and from the looks of them some of the oldest, in his personal collection. Some of them were in good honest English, some in German or French or Eye Tally Anne. There were some in Latin, and I was delighted to see one in dear old Éireannach.

Some were in writing that hurt my very eyes to look at, that Abraham told me were Hebrew or Arabian or San Scrit or Japanee.

Abraham had his nose deep in a huge book when I presented myself. He looked up and closed the book with a loud clap, and a cloud of dust went rising up. Abraham looked tired to me, as if he had been studying all the night while I was at Miss Taryn Jilleen O'Casey's digs pleasing Miss O'Casey with tales of the dear old country and suchlike. This made me feel slightly guilty, but I could deal with it, I truly could.

'We face a very difficult foe, John O'Leary.'

'Not the first, Your Majesty, and I'm sure not the last.'

'Ah, good for you. I enjoy your spirit, John. You would never give up a fight, would you?'

'Of course not.'

'Very well, then. I want you to come with me to the Ohabai Shalome Synagogue. We have the chance to perform a supreme act, John. It will involve a supreme risk, as well.'

'And I am your man,' I told him.

Ah, the smile that I received, it warms my heart to recall it.

'Very well.'

He used his arms to raise himself to his feet. He was wearing a black coat and dark woolen trousers, a white shirt and an embroidered vest of gold and red and green. We walked together from the library to the front parlor. He told me to go fetch the shillelagh that my friends in the Base Ball club had given me, and I did as he asked even though I was puzzled as to his reason. Even before I could move he called out something in Chinee and Xiang Xu-mei came trotting in from her domain.

Abraham said something to her in Chinee and she said something back and he said something else, shaking his fist not at Xiang Xu-mei but in the air. Xiang Xu-mei stamped her foot and shouted something back. Abraham was red in the face. Xiang Xu-mei started to cry.

Finally she disappeared, then returned carrying a fine-looking bowler hat and a walking stick and an odd-looking little pouch with some fringes hanging down from it. I had never seen Abraham ben Zaccheus carry a walking stick before. This was a splendid one, of polished ebony with writing on it in Hebrew. I recognized the letters even though I could not for all the wealth in the world tell you what they meant. The head of the walking stick was shaped almost like a crown, that I swear was finest gold, with more Hebrew writing on the top of it in raised letters. There was even a ferrule, of gold as well.

A pretty penny that stick must have cost His Majesty, unless it was a gift from some of his loyal subjects, all the Hebrews of San Francisco and of the Earth.

Abraham ben Zaccheus gestured and I opened the door and stepped back so he could precede me. We stood outside on the stoop, watching the late afternoon mist creep up Rooshian Hill. We marched to the carriage house and I swung the doors open. Abraham climbed into his electric carriage and in a trice we were heading down Rooshian Hill, bound for the Ohabai Shalome Synagogue.

Father Phinean had told us in St. Padraic's Church in Kilkee that we were never to set foot in any kind of evil temple, be it Buddhist or Hindoo or Mooslim or one dedicated to somebody called something like Zorro Aster. But the two great sins we were to avoid were stepping inside a Protestant Church or a Hebrew Synagogue. One foot planted, one breath drawn in a Protestant Church or a Hebrew Synagogue and Jesus Christ Himself would leap down off His Cross and pierce us through our evil hearts with a foot-long thorn torn from His Holy Crown.

I remember as a lad being terrified of ever going to the city for fear that I might be lured into a Protestant Church or a Hebrew Synagogue and being pierced through the heart with a foot-long thorn wielded by Jesus Christ Himself. Rogan Doherty and me used to scare each other blue by describing the terrible things that would happen to us someday because sure as the river flows, we would one day find ourselves in the city and some wicked Protestant pastor or Hebrew rabbi would tempt us into his Church or his Synagogue and then Jesus Christ Himself would come charging out from the sacristy and stab, stab, stab, and Rogan and me would fall to the floor with our hearts pierced by the sacred thorn, spurting blood all over the carpet and dying while Jesus Christ Himself stands there laughing and pointing at us and jeering, 'Father Phinean warned you, you evil boys, Father warned you and you wouldn't listen, and look at you now, bleeding and dying here in a Protestant Church or a Hebrew Synagogue and now you're sorry, aren't you, Rogan Doherty and John O'Leary, aren't you?'

And here I was sitting all fine and spiffed beside His Majesty King Abraham ben Zaccheus of the Hebrews on my way to the Ohabai Shalome Synagogue on Bush Street in San Francisco.

It's a grand building, I can tell you. Two steeples, not just one, and arches and pillars and lovely stained-glass windows, but the windows have no pictures of the Blessed Savior or his

Virgin Mother or any of the Saints. Instead they have patterns like one of them kalidie-scopes that the little children like to play with, all pretty colors and patterns and suchlike but not a picture you can see.

Amos bar Kiva met us at the door and waited while Abraham ben Zaccheus opened that little parcel that Xiang Xu-mei had given him before we left the house. He took off his bowler hat and put on one of those little yarmee kees that Hebrews wear, and he put a white shawl with some blue stripes on it around his shoulders and he muttered something I couldn't understand, almost like Father Phinean at the secret part of the Mass, and the three of us, King Abraham and Mr. bar Kiva and yours truly made our way into the Synagogue.

It wasn't so different from a church at that, save there was no image of our suffering Savior up on the wall and no statue of his blessed Mother to be seen, but we didn't stay in the chancel or whatever the Hebrews call it very long. We headed for a doorway at the other end

133

of the building and Amos bar Kiva said, 'The kitchen is downstairs. There's a dinner tonight and the women are preparing the food already.'

I could smell the cooking myself, and a delicious odor it was, I can tell you. There's a lot of fish consumed here in San Francisco, not surprisingly for a city with so much water around it and so many fisher-folks making their living off the bounty of the sea. The Hebrews won't touch the tasty bay shrimp or fine Dungeness crabs that other San Francisco folks enjoy, but they are fond of all the finny folk and they make them up in delicious ways with all sorts of fine sauces. Yes, indeed!

Amos bar Kiva ushered Abraham ben Zaccheus and myself through the doorway and onto a landing. We looked down a flight of stairs. 'You see,' he said, 'this is where the three women disappeared. The stairs lead downward, then there is a landing and a turn, then they continue down to the kitchen.'

'How many steps?' Abraham asked.

'Twelve.'

'All right.' Abraham asked Amos and myself to wait where we were. He made his way down the stairs, out of our sight. I heard the voices of women greeting him and Abraham answering in a language I'd never heard even my employer use before. I learned later that it was Ladino.

After a bit Abraham rejoined Amos and myself. 'How many steps did you say?' he asked.

'Twelve.'

'So you did, so you did. Wait here, please.'

Again Abraham descended. This time he returned immediately. 'Twelve, eh?'

'Twelve,' said Amos.

'Very well. Amos bar Kiva, please descend the stairway and wait at the bottom. Do not permit any of the women to leave the kitchen. But before you go, I want you to lock the door behind you. No one may enter or leave this section of the temple. Can you do that for me, Amos?'

Amos assented. He pulled a ring of very large keys from his pocket and turned one in the doorway behind us.

Then he made his way down the stairs. I heard him go.

Abraham put his hand on my shoulder. 'John O'Leary, I am going to rescue those women and their unborn children or die in the attempt. Die, or something far worse. I want you to remain here. Keep your eyes peeled and your ears open. If I call for you, will you come to my aid, even at the risk of your own safety?'

'You mean the risk of my life, Abraham.'

'I mean more than that, John. I mean at the risk of your soul.'

I was still holding the Base Ball shillelagh in my right hand. I shifted it to the left. Abraham held his ebony-and-gold walking stick in his left hand. We clasped right hands, then Abraham turned and started slowly down the stairway. I listened to his progress. He took six steps, then a seventh. At that point he disappeared from my view.

For all that I'd promised to come to his aid if he needed me, I will confess that I disobeyed my employer and followed him partway down the stairway.

Abraham was standing on the landing beyond which the stairway took its turn. As close as I could tell, he was standing on a single slab of black paving slate, what they call hereabouts flagstone. He held his stick by its head and placed the ferrule against the slate. He drew a pattern and stood in the middle of it.

In a loud voice he called out something in Hebrew, then he repeated it — or something that sounded like it — in another language, and then in another, over and over, coming at length to the dear Éireannach, and finally in English. What he said made me shudder. It was this:

In the name of the Sublime One, I command you, Impelluris, Upalluris, Enlil and all you foul demons and so-called gods, and all you Issirra and all you foul demons, to appear and yield up the woman Joaquina Na-Hagid and her innocent unborn one, and the woman Liviya Navon ibn Gabirol and her innocent unborn one, and the woman Nitza Shazar-Suleiman and her innocent unborn one. Hear me, you evil ones, in the name of the Sublime One, I command you!

Abraham reversed his walking stick and with its golden head he smote the rock he stood upon.

At this point there rose from the Earth beneath the synagogue a roaring and a rumbling. The building shook as if the Earth itself was trembling and preparing to quake mightily and a voice so loud it shook the synagogue shouted:

Begone, Hebrew fool, the women you may have but the children will be mine to use for my great work!

Then in a loud voice Abraham called out something in Hebrew, then he repeated it — or something that sounded like it — in another language, and then in another, over and over, coming at length to the dear Éireannach, and finally to English. What he said made me shudder. It was this:

In the name of the Creator, of I-Am-Who-I-Am, I command you, Impelluris, Upalluris, Enlil and all you foul demons and so-called gods, and all you Issirra and all you foul demons, to appear and yield up the woman Joaquina Na-Hagid and her innocent unborn one, and the woman Liviya Navon ibn Gabirol and her innocent unborn one, and the woman Nitza Shazar-Suleiman and her innocent unborn one. Hear me, you evil ones, in the name of the Creator, of I-Am-Who-I-Am, I command you!

A second time Abraham smote the rock he stood upon with the golden head of his walking stick, and the stick broke in two.

A light flashed up from the rock, bathing Abraham in its glare, and a roaring like the very ocean sea in the fury of a great storm, and a stench that blasted my nostrils even where I stood, and stung my eyes like the whips of a jellyfish, a stink like a dead kraken that has lain on the beach in the summer sun for days, and now a terrible low voice whispered so I had to strain my ears to hear it, and it said:

Begone, Hebrew fool, the women you may have but the children will be mine to use for my great work!

Abraham knelt on the rock and shouted out:

In the name of the King the Universe, He who made even the likes of you, I command you, Impelluris, Upalluris, Enlil and all you foul demons and so-called gods, and all you Issirra and all you foul demons, to appear and yield up the woman Joaquina Ha-Nagid and her innocent unborn one, and the woman Liviya Navon ibn Gabirol and her innocent unborn one, and the woman Nitza Shazar-Suleiman and her innocent unborn one. Hear me, you evil ones, in the name of the Sublime One, the Creator, of I-Am-Who-I-Am, of the King of the Universe, I command you!

This time there was no answering voice. The light shone again and the stench came again and the rock where Abraham knelt turned to fog and with a cry Abraham disappeared into the flickering darkness.

He didn't call for my help but I determined to give it anyway. I leaped into the air and fell through the opening after him. I found myself in green water surrounded by creatures with faces like men and bodies like fish, hands like crabs, some of them with scales like carp and some with smooth skins like the bellies of eels and some with hard shells like the crayfish and the crabs of the seas; some with tentacles like the kraken and the devilfish and the stinging jellyfish.

Abraham was there gesturing with his hands and the creatures backed away from him. From among them there appeared three women with bellies like barns and they formed a square with Abraham, holding hand to hand, and they rose through the water and disappeared above us.

The monstrous creatures were all in a circle, swimming and slithering in the round, and in the middle of the circle I stood with my Base Ball shillelagh in my hand, and from among the circling creatures there emerged a great evil one with a head like a cathedral and a single monstrous eye in the middle of its face. Its mouth was filled with row upon row of glistening teeth and it had as many legs as a centipede, each and every one of them tipped with a claw like a pair of cutting shears. It came at me, its one great eye blazing.

I said, 'In the name of the Father and of the Son and of the Holy Ghost, begone!'

The creature did not retreat an inch, did not stop for a moment. It launched itself at me and I swung my Base Ball shillelagh at it and smashed its one great eye like a globe of jelly. The creature drifted away. Mayhap it was dead, mayhap only wounded, blinded, suffering. I cannot tell you. I felt something drawing me upward and in a moment I was standing with Abraham ben Zaccheus and the three Hebrew women with their big bellies.

Abraham said, 'You are the hero of the day, John. Together we have saved these three women, these three precious goddesses of fate, these three who will be mothers and the three new souls who will do God's good works.'

I said, 'But Abraham, your holy stick. It was your scepter, was it not? And it was smashed and lost, its gold head and all.'

Abraham said, 'John Fergus Tiernan O'Leary, it was just a stick. I've a closet full at home. And now, I think we'll be invited to stay for dinner with our friends.'

We were standing at the top of the staircase. I looked down and there were twelve steps and no landing and no turning. The landing would have made thirteen steps but now there were only twelve. The smell of the food from the kitchen was lovely indeed.

'Will Xiang Xu-mei not expect us at Rooshian Hill?' I asked.

Abraham said, 'No, I told her we would be late. But what about your friend on Telegraph Hill?'

'Miss Taryn Jilleen O'Casey? Why, do you think these good people would welcome her as well, for dinner?'

'I'm sure they would, John. I'm very sure. I think you should go now and fetch her.'

'I think I'll do just that, Your Majesty,' I told King Abraham ben Zaccheus. And I made my way to Telly Graph Hill to Miss O'Casey's apartment, and Miss O'Casey was most pleased to accept my invitation for dinner.

Ankareh Minu

Captain Samson always kept a neat desk. The glass covering was spotless. As Rebekkah stood rigidly facing Samson she could see his neat suit, his perfectly knotted tie, his craggy features and razor-cut steel gray hair reflected in it. She knew that her midnight blue sergeant's uniform was in good order, her gold badge carefully polished, her own jet-black hair trimmed and combed to perfection. Even so, she felt shabby compared to the captain.

The commander's chin bobbed a fraction of an inch. 'Close the door, Sergeant ben Zaccheus, and sit down.' When she had complied he resumed. 'You know how political this city can be. You know when the supervisors say jump, we can only ask how high.'

Rebekkah didn't respond except with a slight nod of her own.

'Did you watch last night's meeting of

the Board of Supervisors?'

'On TV, sir.'

'You know that we're taking a beating over this series of fatalities by fire.'

'Yes.'

'Supervisor Moran really let us have it. And you know why, of course.'

'Speak freely, sir?'

Samson smiled. 'Taping system's turned off, Sergeant.' Rebekkah watched, waiting to see if Captain Samson would allow himself a smile. He almost did. Then he slid the case folder across his desk.

Rebekkah opened it. There were incident reports and gruesome photos.

'What do you see, Sergeant? What makes this case unique?'

Rebekkah pursed her lips. She'd been a San Francisco cop for almost a dozen years, since she was a fresh-faced kid out of SF State. All her pals were eager to get down to Silicon Valley or up to the Financial District and show that women can rise as high and make as much money as men. When Rebekkah announced her intention of becoming a cop she got back a combination of sympathetic, baffled, and slyly knowing looks.

She'd seen enough cold corpses in those years, and in the Tenderloin, enough living corpses, to feel only a little shock. 'The bodies are all burned. But none of the incident scenes show any fire damage.'

Captain Samson nodded. 'I knew you'd spot that. Good. But, Sergeant, what does it mean?'

Rebekkah poked her thin, cleft chin with a fingertip. 'First thought, Captain. Somebody's killing people and burning the bodies to disguise their identities or the cause of death, or both. Second thought. File shows each body found in a different location. Identification by dental records, each one found in his own home. All male. Mixed ethnicities.'

'Yes, good. You know how to read a file. However . . . ' He opened a desk drawer, drew out a manila envelope and handed it to Rebekkah.

'Contra Costa County. We generally have good cooperation from them, but this one must have fallen through the cracks. Somebody over there finally woke up and sent this to us.'

Rebekkah studied another crime scene photograph, another blackened corpse. She turned to the Medical Examiner's report. This victim was a female, although you couldn't have told that from the photograph.

Captain Samson asked, 'Where does that get us, Sergeant? Do you have any ideas? Are these cases connected?'

'About a week apart. Might be some kind of nut. Somebody who has to kill every Thursday night because his mommy and daddy made him go to church and miss his favorite cowboy show. But I don't think so. This is nasty. And it's going to be tough. And based on last night's performance, Supervisor Vincent Moran is really pounding us over this.'

'Why? They're not concentrated in his district. They're scattered all around the Bay Area. Mostly here in the city, but here's one in Marin, one in San Mateo, Oakland, Moraga. Why Moran?'

'Good question, Sergeant. Suppose you visit Mr. Moran. Tell him you're hot on the case. No, that's not the right way to put it. Anyway, flash the badge, show the colors, let him know that the department is putting its full resources into this one and we'll keep him fully informed.'

Rebekkah drew a deep breath. 'Captain, politics is politics. I need to know, sir, are you really putting me in charge of this case or do I just go hold the Major's hand?

Samson grinned and shook his head. 'You're not afraid to ask tough questions, are you, Sergeant? Okay, fair is fair. Yes, you're really in charge of this. You'll get whatever support you need. What do you want?'

'For starters, Sir, I just want my partner. Officer O'Leary.'

'Irish Jim O'Leary?' The grin widened. 'You and he go way back, don't you?'

'Actually, our families do.'

'Done. Go.'

* * *

Hall of Justice to City Hall was a five minute jaunt across downtown San Francisco. In Supervisor Moran's outer office a sharply attired Asian woman looked up from her computer keyboard and smiled at Rebekkah. Her eyes flicked to the metal strip on Rebekkah's blouse. 'Sergeant ben Zaccheus, Mr. Moran is eager to chat with you.'

Rebekkah returned her best *We're here to protect and serve* smile.

Supervisor Moran's office was filled with memorabilia. A Presidential citation for his service in Iraq and another for time in Afghanistan. A Silver Star, a Bronze Star, a Purple Heart. Photos of a boyish Lieutenant Moran with General Powell, of an older Major Moran with General Petraeus, of Vincent Moran kneeling in front of a primitive structure, surrounded by ragged, admiring Afghani children, of Moran surrounded by his buddies, of Moran lying in a military hospital bed grinning bravely while a worried-looking woman — his wife? — sat by his bedside holding his hand.

And a framed photo that Rebekkah recognized from a recent copy of the San Francisco *Chronicle* of Supervisor Moran shaking hands with the Governor himself in front of a sign that read, *Vince Moran for United States Senate — The People's Hero, the People's Fighter!*

Oh, yes. Supervisor Moran had his eye on the prize, all right. Not yet forty, a term in the Senate, an easy re-election, and the sky's the limit.

He stood up and extended his hand. The expression on his face was either that of a seriously concerned man or a man very adept at feigning serious concern.

'Sergeant, ah, ben Zaccheus. Thanks for coming over. I know you must be very busy.'

Oh, this guy was good!

Rebekkah nodded. Next he would offer her a seat.

Yep.

'I don't believe in politicians interfering in public safety operations but I also feel a definite responsibility to the voters who put me where I am. And, as you know, this series of incendiary fatalities is threatening to get out of hand.'

'I'm aware of that, sir.'

'Is the department doing anything? I've already talked with the chief and got back the usual line about available resources, concern for the public, blah, blah, blah. That's why I asked him to have someone who's actually working the case come and talk with me.'

'That's why I'm here, Supervisor.'

'You're newly assigned to this case?'

'We've had people working on it, Supervisor. I've read the crime scene reports, forensics, medical examiner's documents. Captain Samson feels that he needs an experienced officer to pull everything together.'

'And that's you, is it?'

'Yes, sir.'

He didn't look happy but at least he didn't say anything about sending a girl to do a man's job. Instead he said, 'I want to be kept informed regularly, Sergeant. I know your chain of command goes up through the Detective Bureau to the Chief's office to the Commission. I'm not trying to shortcut them. But if this case gets out of hand — so far, the media have played it down, they've treated each case as a separate incident, but there's no way they won't connect the dots. And pretty soon. We don't want another Zodiac or Night Stalker, Sergeant. This is urgent.'

She got away as quickly as she could. She made her way back to the Hall of Justice, downloaded information on the case to her laptop, and headed for home.

She shared an apartment on Dolores Street with Officer O'Leary, Liam Francis Xavier O'Leary. Their families had been together in San Francisco for over a century, since a young immigrant, John O'Leary, had answered a want ad in a cast-aside newspaper and gone to work for the famed Kabbalist and psychic detective Abraham ben Zaccheus. It was Liam's night to deal with dinner and he took Rebekkah to a Spanish restaurant within walking distance of their apartment. They shared *Rioja* and *tapas*, flan and espressos and rich, dark chocolates with golden liquid centers.

Afterwards, at home, Liam built a fire. They settled opposite the dancing flames to drink golden *tsikoudia* brandy from Crete and talked about the case. Liam O'Leary was intrigued by Supervisor Moran's interest in the killings. 'You think he wants to ride this into the Senate?'

Rebekkah nodded. 'I think that's part of it. He's got to win the primary first, and something like this could get him over the old San Francisco liberal, soft-on-crime, brie-eating business. He's pushing his war record, too. That'll be big in the Central Valley. Wounded veteran. Tough on crime. Social moderate — at least by local standards.'

'So we bring in some wacko who gets his jollies burning people to a crisp and Major Moran goes to Washington. As simple as that.'

'Not as simple as that.' Rebekkah stared into the fire as if hypnotized. 'I don't know, Liam. I picked up something else.'

'You don't mean a clue.'

'No.'

'Right. You felt a vibration. A cold breeze, a whispered word, things that go bump in the night.'

'Don't start, Liam. You know how I feel about you, but just don't start.'

He reached for her hand. 'I'm sorry, Rebekkah. I know you believe in — well, what you believe in. Not for me to say it's all nonsense. What was it that you got, and what do you want to do with it?'

'You don't mind working this case with me? I asked Captain Samson and he okayed it, but if you're uncomfortable you can get off it.'

'No, Rebekkah. You're a ben Zaccheus and I'm an O'Leary and we've both a tradition to carry on. Just tell me what you want to do.'

'I want you to come with me tomorrow. We're going to visit the crime scenes, some of them anyway.'

'Forensics and Crime Scene kiddies not good enough?'

'You know there's no substitute for walking over the ground, Liam.'

'That I do. But, Rebekkah, now I'm the one who senses that there's something more to your thoughts.'

'What do you think?'

'Ah, sweet sergeant of my heart, you want to hear that ghostly whisper in your ear. *'Twas me wicked nephew what done me in, oo-woo, oo-woo.*'

'Maybe.'

154

'And then?'

'Then I want to go somewhere else for a while. I'd like you to drive with me.'

'Of course, me sergeant.' He drained the last of his *tsikoudia* and placed the empty snifter carefully on the low table. 'Well, unlike you high and mighty sergeants, we patrolmen work for a living. I'm tired and I'm ready to retire for the night.'

'You go ahead, Liam. I want to think about this for a while.'

She refilled her brandy snifter and sat warming the thin glass between her palms, her feet on a hassock, inhaling the brandy fumes rather than imbibing the fluid, gazing into the fire.

The flames had a hypnotic effect, or maybe it was the *Rioja* she'd had with her dinner and the *tsikoudia* she'd sipped and the fumes she'd inhaled after Liam left the room. The red and orange shapes formed faces, or seemed to do so. There must have been some sap left in the wood, and some pine knots, for the flames danced and the sap sizzled and hissed incomprehensible messages to her.

The chimney drew well but a sudden gust of wind must have swept in from the Pacific, driving a small puff of smoke back into the room. Rebekkah breathed in its odor. Her eyelids drooped until the dancing flames filled her vision and the sound of the whispering, bubbling sap filled her mind.

She was jolted awake by the explosion of a pine knot. The empty brandy snifter had fallen from her hands and rolled across the carpet. She drew a deep breath, pushed herself erect and retrieved the snifter. She set it back on the table and stretched out on the sofa and slept.

If she dreamed she did not recall the experience when she was awakened by the sound of Liam O'Leary clattering in the apartment's small kitchen.

'Ah, the sergeant awakens.' He carried a tray from the kitchen and lowered it to the table.

Rebekkah rubbed her temples with her fingertips to get her brain into gear. 'Coffee! Toast! Breakfast fit for a goddess, Liam. And the *Chronicle* to nourish the intellect. An angel thou art!'

He'd opened the *Chron* to the local section and folded it back to expose the story of another death by burning. The tragedy had taken place in a home on one of the worst streets in Hunter's Point, a crime-ridden ghetto. You would have had to look hard to find the report. Crimes in Hunter's Point didn't garner much attention from the media or from the police.

Rebekkah phoned the Hall of Justice and got the shift commander. Crime Scene investigators had already worked the job and the ME had removed the victim's remains. The commander gave her a rundown on the preliminary report. Rebekkah thanked him. She climbed into her uniform. Five minutes later she and Liam O'Leary were headed for Hunter's Point.

★ ★ ★

The woman who answered the door to the victim's apartment could have been anywhere from forty to sixty years old. She wore a stained sweatshirt and jeans, her hair covered with a faded kerchief, her skin an unhealthy shade of burnt sienna. Her cheeks were frighteningly sunken.

'I already talked to police. What else you want of me?'

The apartment was tiny. It smelled of overripe cat litter and stale cooking. There were dishes and pots in the sink and full ash trays and empty wine bottles.

'I'm sorry, ma'am. I know this is a terrible time for you. If you would just go over the facts for me again.'

Liam O'Leary was standing back, clipboard in hand. Out of the corner of her eye Rebekkah observed him studying the room.

'How am I supposed to live now?' the woman was complaining. 'Look at me, woman. I can't work. I can't get no job and I can't work. He was on disability, you know? From the army. He got wounded over there in Afghani. And he got sick. I don't know what that sickness is, a lot of them get it. He couldn't hardly stand up. I had to practically carry him to the VA, he was so sick, and they said it wasn't the army's fault. At least they sent him a check every month. Now what am I supposed to do? I suppose the checks will stop and I can't work and the welfare don't hardly give out money no more.'

She sat down on a dirty sofa and started sorting through cigarette butts until she found one that appealed to her. She struck a match and smoked it.

'If you could just tell me what happened, please.'

There were sounds of voices from the street and thumps. Somewhere nearby an argument broke out; the voices were those of women. They seemed to be competing in cursing each other.

Rebekkah repeated her request.

'What am I going to live on now?' the woman wailed. 'I needed the disability. Now what do I do?'

'Please. Where were you, and where was the victim, please.'

'All right, all right.' The woman poked her cigarette into the pile of butts in the ashtray. Smoke rose slowly from it. 'I was in the bathroom and he was sitting here watching TV. You see that TV there?

Don't get nothing worth watching, just a waste of time. He was watching it and I heard him hollering and somebody else talking.'

'Could you understand what they were saying?'

'I understood my man. He was saying, *Get away from me, get away, I don't want you, go back there, I won't do it.* That's what I heard him saying. He was so weak, you wouldn't think he could talk so loud but he was shouting.'

'And the other voice?'

'I never heard nothing like it. So low, like you could feel it more than you could hear it.'

'A man's voice, a woman's? Could you tell?'

'Too deep for a woman or even a man. Like something from the bowels of hell, that voice. I couldn't understand one word, not a word, but it was nasty, I could tell that.'

'How long did this go on?'

'I don't know. I was scared. I wanted to come and help him but I was too scared. I just stayed in the bathroom. I didn't want that thing to know I was there. And then I heard my man give a loud scream and I heard something like a crack, like something catching fire and I heard my man scream and then just moan and I heard the other thing, the voice, make like laughing only ugly, ugly, and then a thump and I come out of the bathroom and there was nobody there but my man lying on the floor all burned up and dead. And what am I gone do with no more checks every month?'

*   *   *

The house in the Castro was a gaudily painted Victorian, the kind with elaborate gingerbread and a multicolor paint job that wind up in expensive coffee table books on San Francisco architecture. The man who admitted them wore a spotless turtleneck shirt and sharply creased trousers, a bulky cardigan sweater and Birkenstock sandals.

He led Rebekkah and Liam into a parlor and offered them seats upholstered in *faux* tapestry depicting medieval hunting scenes. Tall windows looked out on a tree-lined, hilly street. On the wall Rebekkah saw a framed marriage certificate and an enlarged photo of two men in tuxedos joining hands before a woman in ecclesiastical robes. Another photo showed a young man in an army dress blue uniform, lieutenant's bars on the shoulder boards. It was draped in black crepe.

'Would you like an espresso? Chamomile with lemon? Is it too early in the day for a glass of wine?'

'Tea, please. You're very kind. It's chilly today.'

Rebekkah could see into the kitchen from her seat. It was brightly tiled. There was a large work table and a Wolf stove.

The man brought the tea service on a polished tray. He poured for them all.

'I suppose you want to know about my husband's death.'

'Please.'

'I'm sorry, there's really very little I can tell you. I was at work when it happened. I work on Montgomery Street. I usually get home by seven but I was working late

162

that night. I phoned to see if he was home yet and he was, he said he was making something special for dinner. I said I'd get away as soon as I could but it might be a while.'

He had seemed perfectly composed but he lowered his face suddenly into his hands. When he looked up again his cheeks were wet. He found a hand-kerchief and wiped his face. 'I'm sorry.'

'Of course.'

'I can deal with it sometimes. I put in a lot of hours at work. My friends come by and try to help. We had a lot of friends, you know. A lot. But every now and then — '

Rebekkah waited for him to resume.

'All right. All right, yes. Go ahead, please. Ask away.'

'In your own words, then.'

'When I got home I brought a little gift, a Scharffen Berger chocolate bar. They're the very best, you know. Pricey but worth it. It was a token of affection we used to have. When one of us wanted to apologize for some little thing, he'd bring home a chocolate bar and we'd break it in half

163

and share it and make up.'

He leaned forward, lifted the teapot and refilled Rebekkah's cup. Liam had hardly touched his.

'Would you rather have coffee, officer? No? All right.'

He took a breath and blew it out. 'He didn't come to greet me. I thought he was really angry, I was so late and he'd made us a fancy dinner. But then I came into this room. This very room. And there he was, on the floor. Black and dead. He was still — '

He stopped and shook his head. He was wracked by a sob.

' — smoldering.'

There wasn't much more. The neighbors hadn't heard or seen anything untoward. There was no fire alarm or police call. Just a man turned to a blackened corpse.

★ ★ ★

There were witnesses to the next one. The death took place at two in the morning in the middle of People's Park in Berkeley.

Members of the permanent homeless community had built a campfire and were sitting in a circle. The guitars had been broken out, a variety of voices were singing fragments of songs their owners had grooved to three decades before, bongs and joints and bottles were making the rounds.

A bearded man clad in a warm army jacket, jeans, and worn combat boots jumped to his feet screaming. The singing stopped and the guitars fell silent as he danced in a circle around the campfire.

'At first,' a visibly pregnant woman with a child in each hand recounted, 'at first, I thought he was doing a war dance. You know, like an Indian war dance. He was jumping around, he started going *woo, woo, woo,* like in the movies, you know, and then I thought I saw somebody next to him. I thought he maybe came down out of that tree over there, I don't know, or out of the sky, maybe he was in one of them black CIA helicopters, they come over here all the time, you know?'

'Yes, please continue.'

'Oh, you mean about — well, this other

guy, I don't know, he must have had one of them invisibility cloaks that they have now, you know, he looked all furry or weird, I don't know, I think he maybe had wings and he was burning and he grabbed the poor guy, hugged him and they burned up together, they looked like a holy picture or something, you know, only not a halo, real flames, and then he dropped the poor guy and he faded out and the other guy fell on the ground and thrashed around a little, people were trying to help him but he just died. And they came and took him away. Probably was the CIA, I think.'

And that was the best witness at People's Park.

★ ★ ★

It was an unconventional working arrangement to say the least. On the job they were sergeant and patrolman, case officer and subordinate. Rebekkah made the decisions and led the investigation, Liam did the scut-work, took notes, navigated unfamiliar routes. They wore uniforms or plainclothes as the situation indicated.

In the evenings they relaxed. Sometimes they discussed the news of the day, colleagues at work, plans for their future. At the moment, the biggest issue was whether to get one cat or two. The most urgent was what to do about dinner. It was Rebekkah's night to decide and she chose a favorite robata bar that served the freshest sushi in the Mission.

Over kaiten-zushi and unfiltered saki Liam asked if Rebekkah thought they were getting anywhere with the incendiary murders. 'I don't see any pattern, myself,' he admitted, 'but maybe your voices will tell you what's going on.'

She shook her head. 'Not yet. I'm still looking for a pattern, Liam. And I don't see one. All the victims are male, at least so far. Black and white, rich and poor, gay and straight. Geographically scattered. No business connections I can see.'

She lifted a tekka-maki, dipped it in a mixture of wasabi and soy sauce, and popped it in her mouth. She washed it down with a sip of hot herb tea.

'Tomorrow, though, something different.'

'And would my leader be so kind as to inform me as to the battle plan?'

'Moraga.'

'Ah, the poor folks. And how will that be any different from the survivors we've visited so far?'

'First female victim.'

They finished their meal and walked back to the apartment on Dolores Street. They climbed the old stone stairway from the sidewalk and Rebekkah put the key in the lock. She paused before turning the key. Finally Liam reached and took her hand, assisted her in opening the lock. They went upstairs.

'It's a warm night and your hand was very cold,' he remarked.

'I felt something.' She was pale.

'It's this place, isn't it?'

'Do you know what was here before — before these buildings went up?'

'It never bothered me, Rebekkah. They're old buildings. Pre-quake.' Everything in San Francisco is either pre-quake or post-quake. That's the kind of city it is.

'It was the old Hebrew cemetery. *Gibbath Olom*. The Hills of Eternity.'

'A lovely name for a place of rest,' he said.

'They moved it to Colma. Land here was getting too valuable. Why leave it for the dead when you could sell it to the living?'

'That must have been a long time ago.'

'I heard the story from my mother. They opened it in 1861. There were Civil War dead buried here. Closed it in 1888 and moved all the graves to Colma. All the graves they could find. Nobody knows if they found them all. There may be dead Jews living under our feet.'

'You don't mean that.'

'What?'

'Living. Dead Jews living under our feet.'

'Did I say that? Well, you know what I meant.'

'Your ancestors?'

'No. Abraham was the first of my family to come here and he didn't die until 1907. Post-quake.' She made a little sound that might have had some laughter

169

in it, but not much.

The conversation lapsed and they turned on the TV and watched an old *Streets of San Francisco* episode in rerun, giggling at the silly plot and the low-budget production. It was great fun. They cracked a couple of Kirin beers just to keep in the spirit of the night, then went to bed.

★　★　★

Moraga was across the bridge and through a tunnel and the house they were seeking was up a series of hilly, winding roads.

The house was modern, attractive, clearly well kept. All on one level, as if designed for occupants whose knees were not as supple as they had once been. There was lush landscaping and a three-car garage. The door was down and none of the vehicles were visible. There was a circular driveway covered with sparkling white pebbles that looked as if each one had been washed and polished that morning.

The occupants were a retired couple and they were expecting the visit. Rebekkah and Liam were ushered into an airy living room. There was a fireplace with a gas log but it was not burning. Family photographs were ranged on the mantle. Mr. and Mrs. in much younger days, he with an Afro and a beard; she in a long dress, wearing granny glasses. Another, looking a few years older, he with shorter hair and a moustache, she in jeans and a Greek sailor's cap. Then the two of them with a baby. He looking proud, clean-shaven, respectable; she, maternal and joyous. Pictures of the girl growing up. Then one with him in business suit, her in flowery dress, their daughter in cap and gown. And finally their daughter posing proudly in army uniform, an airborne patch on her cap.

'That's our story,' the mother announced.

'I didn't mean to stare,' Rebekkah apologized.

'It's all right. We loved her very much.'

The father, now white-haired, wearing casual clothes, added, 'We were proud of her. Very proud.'

'She was in the army?' Rebekkah asked.

'I don't know why she enlisted,' the mother said. 'I couldn't understand it. I think — maybe she wanted to follow in her father's footsteps.'

'You served?' Rebekkah asked.

'I was in Vietnam.'

He did not seem eager to talk about that.

'She may have thought we were disappointed, I was disappointed, that we never had a son. I wasn't. I couldn't have loved her more, I couldn't have been happier. But she may have thought that.'

Rebekkah consulted her notebook. 'She died more than a year ago. She was the first in this series of deaths. I hope you'll tell me as much about it as you can.'

The father made a sound and got to his feet. He said something unintelligible and left.

The mother said, 'He's not over it. Neither am I. Do you have any children, Sergeant? No? Then you can't understand. I'm not over it either, but I can put up a better front. See?'

She managed a ghastly smile.

172

'She had a degree from Berkeley. She could have done anything she wanted. She had a boyfriend, too, a fine boy she met in school. But she wanted to do this thing. She went to Afghanistan and came home without a scratch. She said she liked the army, liked the sense of belonging that it gave her. She made sergeant, then they sent her to OCS. You understand OCS? Officer Candidate School? She passed with flying colors. She was a lieutenant. But she always had to challenge herself. She volunteered to be a paratrooper. She was on a training jump. They take them up in helicopters now. She jumped out and something happened. Nobody knows what. She seemed to burst into flames halfway to the ground. It took less than a minute. She was fine when she jumped and she was — she was dead before she reached the ground.'

★ ★ ★

'They got to you, didn't they? The mom and dad?'

173

Rebekkah and Liam were in the Dolores Street apartment.

'They got to me.'

'You want to stay home tonight? I'll make a sandwich, maybe nuke some broth.'

'You're too good.'

He put on some quiet music. He knew her favorite album, Fairport Convention, *Liege and Leaf*. She listened to the voice of the dead Sandy Denny. Liam didn't say anything. She put her head on his shoulder and cried softly for the old couple with the dead daughter.

In the morning she said, 'I'm ready now. I need you to go to Colma with me, Liam.'

'At your command, *mon sergeant*.'

At the relocated Hills of Eternity he waited at a respectful distance while she visited her ancestors. There were many graves in the plot, but she walked from grave to grave, touching the stones, tracing her own direct ancestry, from her father to her father's father to her father's father's father, leaving a pebble atop each to show that a loving visitor had been there.

174

Each stone had only a name and dates of birth and death, the years given since the Almighty had created the world.

Moses ben Zaccheus, 5710–5768.

Jacob ben Zaccheus, 5684–5764.

Isaac ben Zaccheus, 5666–5727.

Abraham ben Zaccheus, 5615–5667.

They rose from their tombs, their voice spoke to her.

'I am your daughter,' she told them. 'To each of you was born a son, through the generations, but now I alone am here. Do not turn from me. Help me, Abraham, Isaac, Jacob, Moses. Help your daughter.'

They gathered around her and spoke ancient words in a language she did not even understand. But one phrase was whispered in her ears, one name. *Ankareh Minu. Ankarah Minu.*

The sky was clear and the air was warm, but she was taken by darkness and cold. When she could move again she went as quickly as she could to Liam O'Leary and he took her back to their apartment.

★ ★ ★

At the Hebrew Institute she found what she was looking for. *Ankareh Minu*. The concept was Zoroastrian. In that ancient and noble religion Ankareh Minu wasn't the devil. The followers of Zoroaster recognized an evil deity, Ahriman, the foe of the good god. No, Ankareh Minu was something else. Not even a demon. It was pure evil, more evil than Ahriman, it was the evil side of human nature.

But why had her ancestors whispered those words to her in the Hills of Eternity? Zoroaster had lived and died thousands of years ago. And Zoroastrianism was a nearly extinct religion, its few remaining adherents concentrated in Iran. What connection was there to the dead in California?

She studied the incendiary deaths. Rich and poor, black and white, gay and straight. Now add female and male. Educated and ignorant, add that, too.

But one had been on disability after being wounded in the army, and died.

One had served proudly, *don't ask, don't tell*, and returned to San Francisco, and died.

One had worn an army jacket, probably his own, kept as a souvenir after serving, and died.

One had served proudly and volunteered for airborne service, and died.

And at the heart of the investigation, the man who had brought pressure on the department, who had prodded Captain Samson into assigning Sergeant Rebekkah ben Zaccheus her tour of the dead, was Supervisor Vincent Moran. Supervisor Moran who soon would be Senator Moran, who might someday be President Moran.

It was not easy to get hold of Moran's service record. He was happy to remind the voters that he was Major Moran, that he had served in Iraq and in Afghanistan. He had the medals to show for it, and show them he did at every opportunity. But as for the full service record — it was not easy to get hold of that but Sergeant ben Zaccheus got it.

Moran had been a lieutenant during the 1991 Gulf War, had served with distinction, won his decorations, and stayed in the National Guard after the war. A decade later, a major now, he volunteered for active duty again. He led troops in the battle of Kunduz in October, 2001. He helped put down the prison revolt at Qala-I-Janghi, supervised soldiers as they routed Taliban at Mazar-I-Sharif.

But what had any of this to do with Ankareh Minu?

Then came the break, the wild break that gave Rebekkah what she needed. It was her day off. Yes, even cops get a day off. Liam O'Leary was on duty at the Hall of Justice, and Rebekkah drove across the Golden Gate Bridge, bypassed the tourist attractions of Sausalito, made her way to a classmate's home in the hills above Mill Valley.

They went for lunch in the community's miniature downtown. They were sitting in a café, eating salads, when an uproar brought the establishment to its feet. A man stood screaming in the middle of the street. Traffic had come to a halt. Rebekkah ran from the café. The man was punching and kicking at an invisible assailant. Passers-by halted to stare and point.

No, not invisible. As Rebekkah approached she saw a cloud of black smoke as tall as a man, swirling like a miniature tornado, sparks and tongues of flame spurting from it.

The victim was caught in the vortex, spinning in opposition to the black and orange whirlwind, both the whirlwind and its victim gaining in speed, smoke rising now from the man.

Rebekkah ran toward the mad duo, her arms spread to encompass them both. She heard herself chanting, not in her own voice, not in one voice, but in chorus, in a language she recognized but did not understand. The chant became an exorcism, a command thundered in the name of the Almighty.

The black and orange whirlwind stretched skyward. Its peak took human form, the form of a naked, aroused male. It dipped and dived at Rebekkah. She faced it, shouting in voices, shouting the Sacred Name of the Almighty.

The whirlwind dived at her. She did not flinch. Closer. She did not cower. She made a sign, the Faravahar Symbol, a sign she had never made, never seen, nor knew, but nevertheless made.

The black whirlwind rushed past her, so close her hair was singed, her skin pained, her clothing blackened. The black whirlwind plunged through the surface of the street, poured into the very earth, and was gone.

Its victim had fallen to the ground. Smoke rose from his clothing and his flesh. His hair was gone, his skin blackened, but he moved and groaned.

When the ambulance arrived Rebekkah showed her badge and rode with the man to the hospital. Rebekkah talked with the man's doctor, learned that he was pumped full of morphine, was being hydrated and treated for his burns. He would probably survive. He could talk, if Rebekkah would be brief. And he might be incoherent from his injuries and the drug.

'Anhareh Minu.'

That was all he would say at first, but he could see and hear and he told his story.

He had been in Afghanistan, had been

under command of Captain Moran. From Kunduz they had fought the prison revolt at Qala-I-Janghi, on to Mazar-I-Sharif, and found themselves in an ancient village called Balkh.

Balkh, where a squad of Captain Moran's soldiers, men and women, hormones pumping from the challenge of battle, the fear of death and the ecstasy of killing, had found a tiny Zoroastrian community, an island surviving in a Muslim sea. The captain himself had led the rapine and slaughter. When it was over the captain and his soldiers had sworn a solemn pact of silence.

But there was no escaping justice. The Ankareh Minu, the evil of the world, had found personification, had found a brother soul in Vincent Moran, and was destroying the soldiers who had destroyed the Zoroastrians of Balkh.

★   ★   ★

'What happened to you, Sergeant?' Vincent Moran pushed himself back from his desk and rose to his feet. 'I heard from

181

Captain Samson that you'd been injured. You — your face. Are you all right?'

'I'm all right, Supervisor Moran.'

'Well, sit down, let me get you something to drink. You've been burned. What happened?'

'No thank you. I would place you under arrest for murder, Supervisor, if I thought I could make the case stick. But I know what's been going on. I know how those people died. I was lucky to save one victim, he's in a burn ward now.'

Moran frowned. 'I don't know what you're talking about. You must be delirious, Sergeant. I can't blame you. I'll see to it that you're put on medical leave. I — '

'No you won't. I know all about Balkh. How many people did you murder? How many women did you rape? How long did it take you to come to your senses?'

'You're the one who needs to come to her senses, Sergeant.'

'No, Supervisor. No. You made a deal with the devil. We're modern people, we don't believe in such superstitious nonsense any more. But Afghanistan isn't a

182

Twenty-first Century country, is it? The past lived there. Ancient gods and demons live there. Zoroaster lived there. Ankareh Minu lives there.'

'Bosh.'

'No. No, Supervisor. You swore your troops to secrecy, and they kept their pledge, every one. Every one until today. You trusted them, you relied on them, but your sights are set high now. You know about opposition research. You've used it against your opponents, you know they would use it against you. And you called on Ankareh Minu and he came. He came when you called and he killed when you commanded.'

The Supervisor stood facing her. He raised his hands, he made a sign with them, a sign like the Faravahar Symbol, but with his hands reversed. He called out in a language Rebekkah did not know, and she called out in the language of her ancestors and in the voices of her ancestors.

A cloud formed outside the office windows and smashed through them, glass shards scattering across the room.

One pierced Rebekkah's cheek and she felt blood spurt.

The being she had seen in the street in Mill Valley stood between her and Vincent Moran.

Moran shouted at the whirling cloud.

Rebekkah opened her mouth to speak and heard only whispers, but the whispers of a congregation of the dead.

Fear spread across Moran's features. Then he was enveloped by the cloud, merged with it, and the cloud rose through the smashed window. Rebekkah stumbled to the window in time to see the black whirlwind plunge into the courtyard, into the earth.

THE END

We do hope that you have enjoyed reading this large print book.

Did you know that all of our titles are available for purchase?

We publish a wide range of high quality large print books including:

Romances, Mysteries, Classics
General Fiction
Non Fiction and Westerns

Special interest titles available in large print are:

The Little Oxford Dictionary
Music Book, Song Book
Hymn Book, Service Book

Also available from us courtesy of Oxford University Press:

Young Readers' Dictionary
(large print edition)
Young Readers' Thesaurus
(large print edition)

For further information or a free brochure, please contact us at:

Ulverscroft Large Print Books Ltd.,
The Green, Bradgate Road, Anstey,
Leicester, LE7 7FU, England.
Tel: (00 44) 0116 236 4325
Fax: (00 44) 0116 234 0205

Other titles in the
Linford Mystery Library:

SERPENT'S TOOTH

Michael R. Collings

Eric Johansson lives in Fox Creek with
his elderly grandmother. But young
Carver Ellis discovers him dead in his
bed, having been severely beaten.
Then, unfortunately for Ellis, the
police officer arriv
already convinced tl
the victim. Victori:
friend down-mount:
work with Deputy l
clear Ellis and unco
died. Can they do
piece of evidence di